I SHALL
ALWAYS
LOVE YOU

I0631631

I SHALL ALWAYS LOVE YOU

SHILPA JAIN

Srishti
PUBLISHERS & DISTRIBUTORS

SRISHTI PUBLISHERS & DISTRIBUTORS
Registered Office: N-16, C.R. Park
New Delhi – 110 019
Corporate Office: 212A, Peacock Lane
Shahpur Jat, New Delhi – 110 049
editorial@srishtipublishers.com

First published by
Srishti Publishers & Distributors in 2018

Copyright © Shilpa Jain, 2018

10 9 8 7 6 5 4 3 2 1

This is a work of fiction. The characters, places, organisations and events described in this book are either a work of the author's imagination or have been used fictitiously. Any resemblance to people, living or dead, places, events, communities or organisations is purely coincidental.

The author asserts the moral right to be identified as the author of this work.

All rights reserved. No part of this publication may be reproduced, stored in a retrieval system, or transmitted, in any form or by any means, electronic, mechanical, photocopying, recording or otherwise, without the prior written permission of the Publishers.

Printed at Repro Knowledgecast Limited, Thane

Love is passion; love is prime
It is earthly, yet divine
It makes you crave; it makes you pine
It knows no boundaries of space and time …

Acknowledgement

I would like to acknowledge my grandparents for making my childhood wonderful and memorable. My parents, especially my late dad, who in spite of his absence from this world is a driving force in my life. My husband, Rajesh, for providing unwavering support through my ups and downs, which have been fairly frequent in my life. My children, Akshay and Aarushi, for loving me back despite my wild mood swings.

Srishti Publishers, especially Mr Arup Bose, for accepting my manuscript, thus fulfilling my long-standing dream of publishing my book.

All those who have been a part of my life for providing experiences that have helped me learn and grow as a person.

And most of all, my readers.

A note from the author

Have you ever wondered who you are? Why you are on this earth? Do you have a purpose… towards yourself or towards the world? Or have you just come to live, breathe, fulfill some worldly duties and experience some worldly emotions? Have you felt something missing in your life? Something deep and meaningful. Something that you haven't been able to fathom because you have been too busy immersing yourself into the wonderful illusions that inhabit this world. Illusions that make you forget the purpose of your journey. Perhaps you have come to fulfill some unfinished business of your soul.

Have you experienced instant and irrational like and dislike towards strangers? You could be willing to forgive even ghastly crimes committed by some, whereas you could develop hatred towards others with minor flaws. Why the difference? Do your souls recognize each other from someplace else? Perhaps you have met each other on some Karmic path.

Seekers of such quests often resort to various meditation and regression techniques that help them take a plunge into their soul and its journey.

For others, the universe plans events to help their souls reach their goals. There is a famous saying, 'When you want something, the universe conspires to make it happen'. Our job is simple – to want the right thing and want it badly enough to remember it across several lifetimes.

Dr Ian Stevenson, a psychiatrist, has scientifically recorded three thousand cases of children who had conscious past life memories. Dr Helen Wanbach, a psychologist, performed a series of experiments dealing with demographic consistencies of past life memories. And her results were encouraging and accurate. Dr Brian Weiss has not only studied past life regression but also future life progression and has written several books on these topics. A handful of well-documented cases of xenoglossia – people under hypnosis speaking foreign words, phrases or language – provides compelling evidence of reincarnation.

Ancient spiritual wisdom of the *Bhagvad Gita* states that a soul is imperishable, and a body is a clothing it changes every lifetime throughout its journey of self-realization. Could introspecting our souls with this knowledge help us resolve our inner conflicts and connect with ourselves? Well, there is only one way to find out.

Knock knock knock …

Shiv, who was sleeping sprawled on his huge bed, moved sluggishly. Mr Saurabh Sanyal, Shiv's father, gently knocked again. Twenty-eight-year-old Shiv mumbled a sleepy, "Come in." Mr Sanyal gestured his personal assistants cum security guards to wait outside. He opened the door, entered Shiv's bedroom and smiled at his sleeping son. He sat at the edge of Shiv's bed and gently stroked his head.

"Happy birthday, son."

Shiv struggled to open his groggy eyes and replied, "Thank you dad."

"Am I the first one to wish?"

"Always."

"This is for you," said Mr Sanyal, handing Shiv a set of documents.

Shiv sat up in bed, rubbed his eyes and took the documents from Mr Sanyal. He tore the documents on seeing them, "I am not ready for this dad."

"You are, son. You just aren't aware."

"Not again dad…not today. I am not going to give up my profession to become a businessman."

"You don't have to give it up, son. You can pursue both. This huge business empire is yours. It is waiting for you to take over."

"Next you will want me to marry someone," muttered Shiv.

"Not someone. I want you to marry Saloni."

Shiv sighed and said, "She is not the one for me."

"Then who is? Arjun?"

"Really? You think I am in a relationship with Arjun?"

"No, I don't. At least, I don't want to. I like the guy. I can't function without him."

"Well, he is that kind of a guy," beamed Shiv.

Mr Sanyal let out a sigh and mumbled, "And this is what makes everyone wonder." He spoke louder, "I'll leave now. We have the annual bash today."

"Hmm, I know."

Mr Sanyal composed himself, transforming his poise from that of an affectionate father to an ambitious business tycoon and walked out of the room.

Shiv Sanyal woke up to embrace another glorified day of his successful life. Born with a silver spoon, he had never known struggle or disappointment. However, unlike his father, who was a successful businessperson, he chose to become an artist. He created paintings and sculptures depicting modernism. Shiv had always received accolades for his work and had never known rejection or criticism.

He was the most featured personality in business magazines, the most eligible bachelor in the city and an heir to the most successful business house. He was a rare combination of class, good looks and great physique.

Saurabh Sanyal, Shiv's father, was known as 'Hercules' in the business industry. He had investments in almost all business types and no one dared to ignite his wrath. He was known to make and break businesses by his valued opinions and movement of investments.

Most business houses bought Shiv's creations in order to maintain good relations with Mr Sanyal. In return, Mr Sanyal rewarded these business houses handsomely by investing heavily in their proposals. His love for his son was his Achilles heel.

Shiv had tasted success without any struggle; hence, he did not value it. He had lost his mother when he was a young boy. However, his father had more than made up for the loss. The father and son were very close.

He was aware that most of his artworks were bought by successful business houses because everyone wanted to keep Hercules happy. However, he had no doubt that his work was extraordinary, and that he would have done well anyway. He did not want to hurt his dad's feelings by asking him to back off.

Apart from all this, there was something that always bothered him. It wasn't work-related satisfaction. What was it then?

He got up, removed his T-shirt and stared at his reflection in the bedroom mirror. He was six feet tall and had a light brown complexion. He had an athletic physique, well-toned body, pumped up biceps and washboard abs. His chiselled facial features with expressive deep brown eyes and exotic haircut added to his macho look.

He took a deep breath and stared at the marks on his body. The horizontal mark on his right ankle resembled a deep cut, a very unusual site for being cut. Besides, he had no memory of such an accident. He turned and strained to see the mark on his back. This mark resembled a whiplash. The scar was very light. He felt that these marks had some significance in his life. But what? He fell back on his bed lost in thoughts.

There was another knock on his door. Before he could respond, a sprightly young woman opened the door and barged in. Shiv looked at her and went back to lying down.

She climbed on the bed, hugged Shiv's bare torso and greeted, "Happy birthday, handsome."

Shiv gently manoeuvred her away and smiled. He placed a kiss on her forehead and said, "Thank you, Saloni." He picked up his T-shirt.

The young woman, about twenty-five years old, was his childhood friend. She was slim, fair skinned, about five feet five inches tall, had delicate facial features, and looked like a doll in the short pink dress that she had worn.

She couldn't take her eyes off Shiv's bare body. His masculinity and his stubble made her breathless. Once again, she passionately hugged him to feel his bare body against her own. Shiv graciously freed himself and raised his eyebrows to question her intentions.

She looked at him seductively and said, "I know you have had the most beautiful women in your life, but I am not so bad either. How about a trial?"

Shiv smiled, cupped her face with his palms and said, "You are a very dear friend. I never ever want to lose you. I have known you since you were about three years old. Mentally, you haven't grown much, and I don't want to be involved with little girls."

Saloni tried to look sensuous by moving her hands through her hair and pouting her lips. Shiv chuckled, lovingly tapped her head and walked into the bathroom. Saloni waited for him on his bed, trying to feel his warmth and scent. She had been in love with him since she was fourteen. However, Shiv had never responded. He only thought of her as a dear friend. She would have readily given herself to him at his slightest indication, but he had never taken advantage.

Numerous eligible men had tried to woo her, but she had never given them a thought. She felt strangely connected to Shiv. She did not understand or analyze her feelings for him and felt it was love.

Watching Shiv go around with his girlfriends had always been a very painful experience for her. She had cried herself to sleep at several occasions and celebrated each of his break-up. After each of his break-up, she had tried to comfort him, hoping to receive love on the rebound. However, she was always disappointed. But she never gave up hope. She believed he would one day realize that she was his true love.

"Can I be your date tonight?" she shouted so that he could hear her in the bathroom.

"Sorry dear," he promptly replied. "Dad is my date tonight."

"Oh yes! My bad."

"You could ask Arjun," Shiv shouted back.

She thought about it, but shoved away the thought. Arjun was a nice good-looking guy, and she sort of liked him, but not enough to go out with him.

"What about lunch?" she asked.

"Saloni, sweetheart, can I get some space to dress. I'll call you in as soon as I am done, I promise."

"Okay, I am leaving... for now."

She went out of the room and busied herself in overseeing the preparations of the annual bash. Mr Sanyal was very fond of Saloni. He thought of her as a well-cultured classy girl who truly loved Shiv. He wished that Shiv would reciprocate. Saloni was polite, peppy, intelligent and caring, and Mr Sanyal had known her from her childhood. She was his friend's daughter.

His friend, Mr Ballad, had approached him several times with a proposal of getting the two married, but Shiv had always declined. Saloni refused to get married to anyone else. Mr and Mrs Ballad were helpless about the situation. They too, like Saloni, hoped that one day, Shiv would change his mind.

Shiv wore a deep V-neck white t-shirt and light blue denims. He carried his brown shades that matched his hair and eye colour and enhanced his suntanned look. As he was combing his hair, there was another knock on his bedroom door.

"Patience Saloni," he shouted.

"It's me," came the reply.

"Hey Arjun, come in."

Arjun came in and hugged Shiv, "Happy birthday."

"Where have you been?"

"Overseeing the arrangements of the bash."

"Thanks for helping out dad, Arjun. I have no inclination and business sense."

"Well, I am not exactly helping out here, it's my job. So quit feeling so bad. I am doing no favours."

Shiv smiled and looked warmly at his loyal and modest friend. He knew that Arjun worked beyond the requirements of his job profile to help his dad.

"How about lunch?" asked Shiv.

"Sure. I can spare an hour or two for my best buddy on his birthday."

Saloni knocked on the open door of Shiv's room, "Am I interrupting the bromance? You guys are walking out on me, huh?"

Shiv noticed the glow on Arjun's face as soon as Saloni walked in.

"I wouldn't dare to. I was just checking with Arjun and was going to ask you to join," said Shiv.

"Join? Incidentally, lunch was my suggestion. No offence, but am I missing something about the relationship you two share?"

"Lines from Hollywood?" asked Arjun raising his eyebrows.

It was a well-known fact that Saloni was an ardent Hollywood fan.

"Sorry for stealing your copyrighted idea," teased Shiv. "May we proceed now? I am kind of hungry."

The trio walked out of Sanyal House. Shiv caringly placed his arm around Saloni's waist. Arjun moved Shiv's arm and placed his own.

All the eight storeys of Sanyal House were lighted up for the annual bash. The party was in the huge hall on the first floor.

Rare artworks from all around the world decorated the cream-coloured walls, and some stood on the floor of the hall. A serene fountain flowed in the middle of the hall and beautiful chandeliers hung from the ceiling. A huge bar was set up in one corner of the hall. Soft music and light filled the room. Guests began walking in from seven p.m.

Shiv was dressed in a light blue shirt, a black blazer and a pair of black trousers. He had gelled his hair and combed them back. He looked like a classic gentleman of the 1900s. Mr Sanyal, a tall sturdy man with a well-trimmed thick moustache and grey hair, was dressed in a classic dark brown suit.

Arjun, tall, fair and athletic, was always clean-shaven. He was very dependable and modest; qualities that made him very likeable.

He had arrived early and was receiving the guests. All the guests were respectfully seated around the numerous tables placed in the hall. Arjun was aware that several businessmen who had arrived were rivals. Therefore, he had placed them at a comfortable distance from each other.

At around eight, Shiv and Mr Sanyal arrived together. All the guests cheered for them.

Mr Sanyal took to the dais and spoke, "Today is the happiest day of my life. Life has always showered me with more than what I deserved. I am grateful to each one of you for bestowing your wishes. Today, both my company and my son have turned twenty-eight. Both my kids have made me proud."

Shiv smiled at his dad and joined him on the dais. "I don't want this to look like a mutual admiration club, but he is the best dad one could have."

His eyes were filled with tears as he hugged his dad.

"Big men don't cry," Mr Sanyal whispered in Shiv's ears.

Shiv straightened himself and opened a bottle of champagne to begin the celebration. Saloni was by Shiv's side in no time. She had worn a wine-red strapless fish cut gown that hugged her svelte body. Her hair was tied up in a high bun. Her wine-coloured lipstick made her look irresistible. She looked ravishing as the colour of her gown reflected on her fair skin.

Shiv kissed her on her cheek and whispered, "You look stunning!"

Her face lit up on hearing the compliment. "Wanna try me?"

He smiled, mildly shook his head sideways and said, "Sweetheart, I am not a Hollywood fan. Besides, you are too sweet for my taste."

"Perceptions are deceptive."

Arjun interrupted and introduced Shiv to several important guests. After a while, Shiv went to the bar to relax. He never really enjoyed such parties. Arjun came and handed him a mask. Shiv looked at him questioningly.

"It's time for the masquerade party. All bachelors and spinsters are moving to the hall on the second floor for the masquerade dance," said Arjun.

Excitement in the air was palpable as all of the young guests were trying out their shiny and glamorous masks. Shiv complied to please Arjun and wore the black shiny mask handed to him by Arjun. It made him look like a superhero with gelled hair.

On the second floor, many ladies lined up to enjoy a dance with Shiv. Arjun too had quite a fan following. He looked great in a dark blue mask that matched his suit. Being chivalrous, Shiv tried to oblige as many women as he could.

A young woman passing ahead brushed against Shiv while he was dancing with Saloni. Shiv felt a sudden gush of emotions as she passed by. He tried to catch a glimpse, but could only see her from behind. She was wearing a black silk gown. He felt sudden unexplainable sadness when he saw her going away. She was being led away by a man.

She had a full figure and waist length silky black curls. Shiv was unable to see her face, but felt sudden pain in his heart as she was leaving. An air of melancholy surrounded him.

He excused himself and followed her. He rushed out of the hall, but the man and woman were nowhere in sight. He hurried down the stairs to reach the compound of Sanyal House. The valet of Sanyal House had brought a black Audi at the gate. The man leading Shiv's mysterious lady was holding the door to the rear seat of the car for her.

A gush of wind blew her hair exposing her beautiful bare back and Shiv could see a scar similar to his on her back. Shiv was astounded on seeing the scar. Just as Shiv was rushing towards the Audi, someone pulled him away. He realized that he had just missed being hit by a fast-moving Mercedes. The black Audi drove away and he turned around to look at his saviour. A dark woman in her sixties with a pleasant and mildly wrinkled face dressed in a white robe was looking at him horrified.

"You almost got yourself killed!" she shouted.

Before Shiv could explain, Arjun hurried out looking for him, "What happened? Is everything okay? I saw you leave in a hurry."

Shiv was still looking in the direction of the black Audi. He straightened himself and thanked the lady. Arjun introduced the lady in the white robe as Ms Devi.

"Mr Sanyal says that Ms Devi has special powers. He has invited her to bless you on your birthday," said Arjun.

"Very well," replied Shiv and bowed his head.

"You are a gentleman, a rare find," she said smiling and affectionately touched his head to bless him.

She closed her eyes and concentrated. After a few seconds, she opened her eyes, took his hands and closed her eyes again. She stood still for a while. Shiv looked at Arjun quizzically. Arjun raised his hand signalling him to be patient. When Devi opened her eyes, she looked enlightened.

"Today is a special day for you, as has been in your previous lives. I am glad I saved you."

Shiv looked baffled. "No offence ma'am, but I certainly do not believe in previous lives and reincarnations."

"I understand. Most don't, but you will come around soon. I am your soul guide and you are my last mission of this lifetime."

Before Shiv could argue, Arjun broke them off and requested Ms Devi to accompany him upstairs.

She lifted her hand and said, "I have accomplished what I have come for. I wish to go back now. Give my regards to Saurabh."

She left in the white Porsche that she had come in. Shiv looked at Arjun, who seemed equally perplexed.

"She is a very well-known psychic and Mr Sanyal often visits her," he said.

"Forget her. Could you find out who left in the black Audi a while ago?"

"Sure," replied Arjun, no questions asked.

Both went back to join the party.

Neither of them had noticed that Saloni had followed them downstairs. She was devastated on seeing Shiv go crazy over a woman he had not even seen. With tear-filled eyes, she introspected her emotions for Shiv. Why did she feel so attracted to Shiv? What did she owe him? Why couldn't she get over him? Was it love or was it something else? Was she confused? She went upstairs, lost in pensive sadness.

After the party, when Shiv was retiring to bed, he heard a familiar knock on his door.

"Arjun, buddy, come in."

Arjun walked in with his neatly-folded coat suspended on his forearm. The upper two buttons of his shirt were undone and the tucking dishevelled. He looked exhausted from the party. Shiv moved to make place on his bed for Arjun. Both friends sat next to each other for a while, blankly staring into the air.

Arjun brought out a cigarette and lighted it.

Shiv was surprised, "Whoa! Whoa! When did you start smoking?"

Arjun exhaled a cloud of smoke and said, "It's just a little vent for…"

"For Saloni?" interrupted Shiv.

"Recently, she spent a lot of time with me, but all she spoke about was you. I love you so much that I can't even hate you for this. What do I do?"

Shiv felt awful for his friend. Smoky silence filled the room for a while.

After a few more puffs, Arjun said, "About the Audi, it belongs to Raj Mittal. He had come in with his special female friend."

"I see," replied a dejected Shiv.

"What is it about this lady? You haven't even seen her. She is with Raj Mittal, so don't play around unless you are serious."

"You know that I have never played around with any of my girlfriends, but it just never worked out."

"Fine. Give me some time to find out about her."

"Arjun, if you had been a woman, I would have been deeply in love with you," said Shiv winking naughtily at Arjun.

"And this is what makes everyone wonder why we are a couple. Anyway, I am glad I am not a woman. I wouldn't have liked my man being involved with so many other women."

They laughed and chatted about their younger days for a while before parting.

"You remember Shalini?" asked Shiv.

"Shalini… can't place her. Oh, yes! The pretty girl you were trying to pursue in junior college?"

"Yes. Her big brother had come with a gang of bullies to thrash me after she complained about my advances."

"What about her?"

"What did you tell her brother? He backed off without harming me."

Arjun was reluctant.

"Come on! You have to tell me today."

"Okay. I was only trying to protect you. I hadn't mastered my martial art techniques back then to fight them off."

"Cut the crap," said Shiv impatiently.

"I told them … that … you were gay, and that it was him you were interested in."

Shiv was flabbergasted.

"I was only trying to protect you. They would have killed you," explained Arjun.

"No wonder I never had a girlfriend in junior college," Shiv murmured.

When Shiv recovered from the shock, Arjun was at the door. He greeted him good night and left in a hurry. Shiv chuckled after he left.

Shiv lay on his bed and tried to sleep. He tossed and turned all night, but couldn't get the vision of the young lady out of his head. Her silky long curls, her full figure, her breast bulge seen from her sides, her round hips and her beautiful back with the scar. The scar made him restless. Is it possible for two people to have identical scars? He became anxious.

He wanted to grab the woman, see her face, take her in his arms, feel her and love her.

He sat up startled and shook the thought out of his head. He had been involved with many women before, but had never been obsessed with any of them. In fact, a few of his women had been obsessed with him and had threatened to kill themselves when he broke up. Arjun had managed to handle each one of them.

For the little time that he slept, he saw strange dreams. He saw erotic sculptures of nude men and women engaged in various sexual acts, nude women in various poses, a nude man embracing his consort. He could see the sculptures very closely, every fine detail and line on them, as though he had created them.

He could not believe the effect the young woman was having on his mind. She seemed to control him. He had to find her.

Shiv was up at dawn, sweating and uneasy. Was it the party? No. He had been to such parties before and no amount of alcohol had this kind of effect on him. Besides, he hadn't had any alcohol yesterday.

He could not get the images of the erotic sculptures out of his mind. He sat in bed, bewildered. He then got up, picked up a bottle of water and went out to his bedroom terrace.

The view from his bedroom terrace on the sixth floor of Sanyal House was spectacular. The magnificent sea opposite the mansion was calm. Its waves were gently crawling towards the sea wall. The road running parallel to the sea was quiet, except for a few morning joggers. One could hear the soft gushing sound of the sea waves during this time of the day. The horizon was a mix of dark blue and orange. He leaned against the railing and watched the morning joggers. He then changed into his gym wear and decided to work out to vent his agitation.

He was unable to concentrate on his workout. While running on the treadmill in the gym located on the seventh floor of Sanyal House, his thoughts kept going back to the woman in black and the erotic sculptures. Were these facts connected? Was there any truth in what Ms Devi had said? He ran faster and faster. The harder he tried to keep his mind off the mysterious woman, the tougher it seemed.

His train of thought was disturbed by the ringtone of his cell phone. It was Arjun.

"Impeccable timing, my friend!" said Shiv.

"Did you sleep well?"

"Nope."

"I thought as much. I got some info on Raj Mittal. The man is married and the woman he brought was his mistress. Do you still wanna pursue her? I suggest you back off now before it's too late."

"It's already too late, Arjun."

"My sympathies then, because Raj Mittal is on a trip to Paris and has taken his mistress along. He is expected to return after eight days, just a day prior to your next exhibition. Don't you need to concentrate on your upcoming exhibition for now?"

"Yes. Thanks for the reminder, Papa," said Shiv.

Shiv felt a sudden gush of jealousy and anger on hearing that his lady in black was a mistress to some other man and was out in some exotic place, seducing him. He was edgy again. He felt his manhood hardening on imagining her seducing him. He began relentlessly punching his boxing bag until his fists hurt. Here I am, obsessed with her, and there she is, ignorant about me, enjoying sexual bliss with another man, he thought.

He thought about his upcoming exhibition. He was almost ready, except for a few artworks that required final touches.

He showered and changed into comfortable track pants and T-shirt and went to the eighth floor of Sanyal House. His workshop was on this floor. All his paintings and sculptures were modern and futuristic. However, in his dream, he had visualized ancient sculptures.

A huge slab of black stone was standing on the floor of his workshop. He made up his mind to create a sculpture of the 'eternal embrace' he had seen in his dream. He picked up his chisel and hammer and began sculpting. Working on the sculpture provided him some relief from his current state of mind. For the remaining seven days, he literally lived in his workshop. The only thing on his mind was the sculpture and the lady in black.

Mr Sanyal was on a business trip and kept in touch through phone calls. He had no clue about Shiv's state of mind. Shiv had been avoiding Arjun and Saloni as well. On the seventh day, both of them forced their way into Shiv's workshop to ensure everything was fine. As soon as they entered his workshop, they were awestruck. Both of them stood facing the latest life-size sculpture created by Shiv.

"It's out of this world!" said Saloni. "I forgive you for the last seven days."

"Shiv, I have never seen anything like this," said Arjun, delighted. "And you created this in just seven days?"

Shiv stepped back to look at the sculpture. He hadn't realized that he had locked himself up for one week. He was only trying to vent out his aggression and disappointment. But now, the wait was over and he would be able to pursue his dream of finding his lady in black.

The sculpture was that of a nude woman with rounded curves tightly embracing a nude muscular man. Their eyes were gazing into each other and their lips were ready to lock. Their hips and legs were intimately close to each other. The man had shoulder length hair and wore a golden headband. The woman wore golden armlets, anklets and a waistband. Both arms of the woman were on the man's shoulders. The man's arms were possessively wrapped around the woman's upper back and lower waist. The slight forward bend by the man and his tensed neck muscles revealed his passion, whereas the facial expressions of the woman revealed her eagerness. The sculpture had beautifully captured and breathed life into a passionate moment of romance.

Shiv stepped ahead and sensuously stroked the bare back of the woman's sculpture to feel the scar.

Arjun tried to distract him by clearing his throat, "Are all the other artworks ready? Do you need help?"

Despite the interruption, Saloni had noticed the passionate stroke.

She raised her eyebrows and commented, "I thought I had to compete only with living beauties. This raises my difficulty to a whole new level."

Shiv ignored her comment. "I am in love with this lady. Can I have a moment with her?"

Saloni let out a sigh and left.

Arjun went closer to Shiv and said, "I thought you were over the lady by now."

"Over? I am getting more and more into her. She is constantly on my mind. Is she back?"

"I wasn't stalking her, Shiv. Let's finish with the exhibition and then we will find out. One task at a time."

Both of them walked to the window of the workshop and stood gazing at the sea.

"Why don't you tell Saloni about how you feel?" asked Shiv.

Arjun bit his lip. "I am not ready for a rejection. I hope someday she will notice my feelings after she is over you. Do you reject her advances because you know how I feel about her?"

"Arjun, I just don't feel that way about her. But to answer your question, I would have backed off for you even if I felt that way. Do you want me to talk to her?"

"Nah! I will, when the time is right," replied Arjun pleased with Shiv's answer. He would have done the same for Shiv.

"I'd be jealous if my girl loved you so much," said Shiv putting his arm around Arjun's shoulder.

Arjun reciprocated Shiv's action and said, "I too am jealous and sometimes wish to thrash you, but I trust and love you too much to do that."

The exhibition was held at Sir Wilson Grey art gallery. Arjun had supervised most of the arrangements. He had prepared the critic and invitee list very thoughtfully. Some very popular national and international artists and celebrities were invited. Mr Sanyal had just returned from his business trip. He was impressed by Arjun's managerial skills and was looking forward to the evening.

Shiv had been up all night giving final touches to his artwork, mostly to his latest sculpture. The artworks were transported to the gallery in the afternoon. Shiv supervised the display of his artworks. There was still enough time for him to go back and return refreshed.

Saloni was in his room helping him choose his look for the evening. She had brought along a beautician to groom Shiv, and he never had a chance to protest. She got rid of his unshaven look and under eye dark circles. He wore a dark brown shirt, light khaki trousers and a matching blazer. His classy casual leather shoes and belt gave him an exotic look.

Saloni wore a dark green halter-neck evening gown with matching emerald studs. She looked ravishing in her smoky green eye makeup and brown lipstick. She stood out in the crowd and proudly discussed Shiv's artworks with everyone.

Arjun managed to steal looks at her from a distance. His heart began racing when he saw her walking towards him. He stood still and watched her while she spoke to him. He was so lost in admiring her that her words seem to drown.

"Is that okay?" were the only words he comprehended.

"Perfect," he replied.

She smiled and walked away with springs in her steps at his approval for whatever she said.

Shiv was busy discussing his art with art critics when Mr Sanyal walked in. Shiv excused himself and took his father around. Mr Sanyal stopped in front of the black sculpture.

"Son, don't give away this masterpiece. I am going to keep it," said Mr Sanyal.

"Sorry dad, but this is mine," said Shiv winking at his dad.

Just then, Shiv sensed something pleasant in the air. He turned around and saw a young lady dressed in a little black dress admiring one of his paintings. Her hair was tied in a high ponytail. He knew at once that she was his lady in black. His heart was beating fast as he raced across the hall to meet her.

Unfortunately, Saloni interrupted him.

"Anish Kapoor, the famous ancient art critic is here."

Before he could protest, she grabbed him by his arm and led him in the opposite direction. Mr Sanyal and Arjun were already playing hosts to Mr Kapoor, who was one of the most honest critics around. Nobody could influence his views on art.

"Hello, young man," he said extending his hand to Shiv.

"It's been a treat to see your work, your original work. It is brilliant. I am glad Arjun sent me an invite and I could make it," said Mr Kapoor.

Shiv looked confused. "I didn't quite comprehend your comment. All my work is original."

Mr Kapoor glanced at the crowd of celebrity guests, artists and journalists that had gathered around him. He resisted disputing, but Shiv insisted.

"Which of my works do you think is not original, Mr Kapoor?"

Mr Kapoor walked towards the black sculpture and said, "This piece here, the pose, expression and even the design on the jewellery is a remake."

"That's impossible!"

Mr Kapoor seemed angry at being challenged and shot back, "Have you ever visited Khajuraho, Shiv? If not, please do."

He stormed out of the gallery and the journalists had a gala time covering this news. They had juice for their papers and magazines.

Mr Sanyal glanced at Arjun who nodded and said, "I'll take care of the media."

Shiv stopped Arjun. "I can handle this. Let them write what suits them. I am going to take Mr Kapoor's advice and visit Khajuraho to find the truth."

Shiv forgot about the lady in black and plodded out of the gallery.

At Sanyal House, he locked himself up in his bedroom and stood on his terrace staring at the sea with vacant eyes. He had never been to Khajuraho and had never seen images of sculptures from Khajuraho. Then, how did he make a replica of a sculpture from Khajuraho? What was the connection? Was it just coincidence? This seemed unfathomable to him. He had to visit Khajuraho to seek the truth.

His cell phone was continuously ringing. Mr Sanyal, Arjun and Saloni were trying to connect with him. He had refused to see them in person. After a few hours of isolation, Shiv picked up his phone. He had a few messages from Arjun. Arjun had made Shiv's travel and stay arrangements for Khajuraho and had left the documents with Mr Bijlani, the chief caretaker of Sanyal House. Shiv replied to the message and thanked Arjun.

Saloni's message read that she was going to accompany him to Khajuraho the coming morning. No! I need to do this alone, he thought.

He called up Saloni. "Hey, did I wake you up?"

"How could I sleep when I know you are in pain? Are you better?"

"Trying not to think about the incident."

"Don't beat yourself up. Everyone knows that Shiv Sanyal is original. You don't need to prove yourself to a bunch of jerks."

"Unfortunately, the world doesn't view me with your eyes, sweetheart. Anyway, I need a break and need to be with myself. I appreciate your generous offer, but this is not the time. I'll see you after I'm back."

After a silent pause, she replied, "Okay, but promise me that you'll take good care of yourself. I will be with you as soon as you need me. I want to hear from you every day. Do you get that?"

"Yes ma'am."

S hiv set out early for Mumbai airport for his flight to Khajuraho. He could hardly sleep all night. He had never been so excited. He was looking forward to visit Khajuraho. The bad publicity hardly mattered to him. He knew he had created an original sculpture, but the coincidence had given a new mission to his boring life. He hoped to find a connection.

He was all over page 3 of all the daily newspapers.

The various captions read:

'Was he ever original?'

'Shiv Sanyal's past works to be reviewed'

'More critics open up about the Khajuraho replica'

'Will Papa Hercules protect his son this time too?'

He looked around and saw a number of travellers staring at him. He nodded politely and proceeded for a coffee. Fortunately, the luxury flight mostly had foreign tourists who did not recognize him. He relaxed during the one-stop journey. When the plane landed, he was all charged up to explore the destination on his own. He hoped that no one would recognize him in Khajuraho.

To his displeasure, as soon as he stepped outside the airport, he saw a young jaunty short-statured man in his early twenties waiting for Shiv with a name placard. The man was dressed in a red shirt, dark blue denims, black gumboots and a stole with printed Khajuraho sculptures smartly wrapped around his neck. Shiv sighed and cursed himself for not instructing his overbearing friend Arjun to leave him alone this time. While passing ahead to meet the guy, he saw one more man standing with his name placard. Arjun is unbelievable, he thought. A backup for pick up too!

He walked up to the man in the red shirt. The stole depicting Khajuraho sculptures seemed to attract him. Shiv introduced himself and complimented him on his stole. The stole had pictures of ancient sculptures of women in various poses such as looking into a mirror, removing a thorn from the leg, tying a girdle, applying kohl, etc. He noted the similarity between the voluptuous figure of the lady in his black sculpture and the women in Khajuraho sculptures. He also noticed that the design on the jewellery was similar to that on his sculpture.

This suddenly reminded him of his lady in black. He had completely forgotten that he had seen her at the exhibition.

He called up Arjun, "Hey buddy, just reached."

"Cool, how are you feeling?"

"Just about okay. Don't worry, I'll come around."

"You sure will," assured Arjun. "I'll settle the heat over here before you get back."

"Don't bother about it Arjun. I called to ask about my lady in black. I thought I saw her at my exhibition. Was she there or was I hallucinating?"

"Oops! She was there Shiv. I had invited Raj Mittal hoping that she would come along, and she did. But after the chaos, it completely slipped my mind. Is she still haunting you?"

"You bet, she is."

"I'll follow up on her."

"Hey, by the way, thanks for the backup pick up," said Shiv, but the call dropped before Shiv could complete his sentence.

He decided against calling back. Arjun tried calling back, but received a no network reply. The pickup guy introduced himself as

Tony. He was a charming fellow and spoke with a local Bundelkhandi accent, which Shiv felt was amusing and endearing.

"How long have you been doing this job?" asked Shiv.

"From as long as I can remember. I breathe, dream, eat and drink Khajuraho stories. There is so much history in every corner of Khajuraho. This will be a memorable vacation for you, sir. I assure that by the time you leave, you will feel that you have met the historical Khajuraho personalities face to face," replied Tony.

He dropped Shiv at a five-star hotel, gave him some illustrative books on Khajuraho history and asked him to just read and relax in the afternoon.

"I'll pick you up at seven in the evening for the light and sound show at the Kandariya Mahadev Temple."

Shiv insisted on paying Tony, but he replied, "Thank you sir, but your friend has more than compensated me."

Shiv frowned and thought that Arjun had really overdone it this time. He checked into his room that had a beautiful temple facing view. From the balcony of his room, he could see some of the western Khajuraho temples. From the distance, it was impossible to see the details of the carvings on the walls of the temples. He wished he had brought his binoculars. He felt a surreal connection with Khajuraho.

He was fatigued due to lack of sleep and decided to skip lunch. Instead, he opened a can of an energy drink and sipped on it while surfing various TV channels. A local Khajuraho channel was on and Shiv settled on the bed to watch it. The channel was playing Indian classical music, and it focused on details of the sculptures of Khajuraho temples. Shiv observed these sculptures scrupulously. When he saw the sculpture that was similar to his, his heart missed a beat. This sculpture evoked nostalgic feelings similar to those stirred by his black sculpture. There was definitely something going on here, he thought.

His phone beeped; he ignored the message and picture received from Arjun. He messaged Saloni that he was fine. She replied almost immediately requesting that he should call her as soon as he was up to it.

He switched off the TV and moved to the balcony outside his room. There was a rocking chair. He carried the books on Khajuraho history given by Tony and settled on the chair in the balcony. The books were stamped 'Khajuraho History Museum'. He read about the historical personalities and incidences of Khajuraho, and saw all the illustrations minutely. The more he read, the more he felt connected to the place.

He gazed at the temples from his balcony and didn't realize when he fell asleep. Some activity at the temple awakened him. It was six p.m. He realized that he was famished.

He showered, changed into a black polo T-shirt and a pair of denims, and proceeded to the hotel restaurant and had his meal.

He then went to the lobby. The elegant ambience and the bright lighting of the lobby were very welcoming. He waited at one of the numerous cozy seating areas and flipped through a coffee table book on Khajuraho sculptures and nearby sightseeing areas. Tony was at the lobby at sharp seven p.m.

"On time, huh?" said Shiv.

"Always, sir. Good evening. I have the tickets for the show."

"How much do I owe you?"

"Your friend has already paid me, sir."

"Of course," replied Shiv, amused.

The light and sound show at Kandariya Mahadev Temple was mesmerizing. It took the viewers through a journey of the history of Khajuraho and its temples. The music, voice and history lingered in Shiv's mind for long after the show was over.

He invited Tony to have dinner with him. Tony politely declined, but Shiv insisted. Tony was a natural historian. He discussed the views of famous people who had visited or written books about Khajuraho. He specially discussed views on various erotic sculptures. Shiv showed

Tony a picture of his black sculpture. Tony looked at it and seemed impressed.

He remarked, "This is amazingly similar to one of the Khajuraho sculptures in the eastern group of temples, except for the colour. Also, in your sculpture, the woman has both her legs together, whereas in the Khajuraho sculpture, the right leg of the woman seems to be a little behind as though pulled by something. That is a very minor difference though."

Shiv was impressed by Tony's perfect observation. He thanked Tony for a wonderful day and looked forward to the next. Shiv's mind was completely clouded by Khajuraho and its history. He had several missed calls from his dad. He called up Mr Sanyal and spoke at length. He felt good after that. He saw the image and message sent by Arjun.

The message read,

Your lady in black, Nysa. Hope this will suffice for now. Rest later.

Nysa, his mysterious lady! She was breathtakingly beautiful with prominent black eyes, full lips and light brown complexion. A small light blemish on her forehead seemed to enhance her beauty. He wondered what Arjun meant by 'rest later.'

He relaxed and slept that night with Khajuraho in his thoughts and dreams.

In his dream, Shiv was transported to a house in the 11th century in southern India, a whitewashed structure built of stones and mud. The entrance of the house was decorated with beautiful paintings of trumpeting elephants on either side.

Inside the house, the women folk were serving dinner to the male members and children of their family. The head of the house was Satya Silpi. He was dining with four of his sons and five grandchildren – three boys and two girls.

All his sons except the youngest, Rudra, were married. Rudra was over twenty-seven years old, which was well beyond the marriageable age in those days. Most of Rudra's friends were married and had children between six to ten years of age. Every evening, the conversation during dinner revolved round Rudra's marriage and future.

Satya began, "Son, look at your brothers. Aren't they happily settled? They have lovely wives and children. They have something to look forward to. Your sisters too are happy and busy taking care of their families. Why don't you want to get married?"

Rudra continued to eat without responding.

Satya continued, "You are the best sculptor in this village. The head architect of Brihadisvara temple has acknowledged your work and employed you as one of the main sculptors at Gangaikonda temple. My friend Surya will be visiting us with his daughter. You have to accept the proposal to marry her. You are well past the age of marriage. People make fun of you. I just want to get over with my last responsibility. Do you understand?"

Rudra ate his food without responding. His elder brother nudged him. Rudra's train of thoughts was suddenly disturbed. He hadn't been listening to what his father was saying.

He said, "Father, I have decided to move to Jejakabhukti."

All his brothers were shocked and dropped the morsels from their hands. The grandchildren too were shocked at their favourite uncle's statement. Rudra's mother was dazed and had to be physically supported by her daughters-in-law.

Satya was furious. "What do you mean?"

"I want to see the world beyond Dakshinapattam. I want to go to Khajuraho."

"What? Why?"

"There is a lot of work going on there. Chandela King Vidyadhara and Grandmaster Sivdutt have invited experienced sculptors from other kingdoms to work at Khajuraho."

All the family members were even more shocked. Satya signalled his daughters-in-law to take the kids to the inner room.

Satya's eyes were blazing. "You have been trained by the architects of Chola kingdom and you wish to work for the Chandelas? We would rather kill ourselves than be called traitors."

"Father, please let me go. Many sculptors from Chandela kingdom have come to our kingdom too. The two kingdoms are promoting exchange of art and culture. Nobody is a traitor. I have even started learning their language from some of the immigrant sculptors."

"I have heard bad things about the culture and sculptures of Khajuraho. You have a pure heart, son. You are too naïve. You will be corrupted by their culture. I do not wish to lose you."

"I understand, father. Trust me, you will never lose me. But please let me go, so that I can find myself."

Satya realized that there was no way he could persuade his son. Hence, he agreed to let him go with a promise that he would return soon. That night, when Rudra was lying in the courtyard of his house and stargazing, his best friend Abhay jumped over the fence to lie beside him.

Rudra smiled and said, "I am going to miss you."

Abhay seemed confused and asked, "Are you dying tonight?"

"Sort of. The new 'me' will be born tomorrow. I finally have something to look forward to. Khajuraho, here I come."

Abhay sat up horrified. "Your father has agreed to let you go? You can't just leave me here."

"Why not? I am not married to you. You are married to the most beautiful woman of this village and you have two adorable kids."

"Yes, the most beautiful woman just kicked me out of her bed. All she cares about is her kids. I need to know a woman more intimately. I long for a woman who would care only about me and my needs."

Rudra narrowed his eyes, "That's very selfish. Shouldn't you too be caring for the kids?"

"I do provide for them, don't I? I have a plan. I'll accompany you to Khajuraho. That way, I'll continue to provide for them and have some fun too. I'll have the best of both worlds. I have heard about the liberty the place provides. Aren't you seeking the same?" asked Abhay.

"You are sick," replied Rudra.

Abhay laughed and went back to lying down and star gazing. Rudra tried hard, but failed to convince Abhay to stay back for his family.

The next day, Satya awakened Rudra by gently stroking his forehead. Rudra looked at him with affectionate eyes.

Satya said, "I always knew that I couldn't hold you back. I knew that someday you would leave us to follow your heart. My blessings are always with you, son."

Rudra was gloomy. "Father, I am torn between my duty towards you and my heart's calling. What am I to do?"

Satya smiled with weepy eyes and replied, "Son, I relieve you from your duty towards me. I have other sons to fulfil those. You are meant to do something special. I can't keep you away from your destiny."

Rudra felt as though a huge weight was lifted off his heart. Year after year, he had suppressed his desire to visit Khajuraho. It was finally going to be fulfilled. The family prepared for his farewell. Various elders of the village guided him regarding the route to Khajuraho. They warned him about various obstacles they could face. A farewell celebration was planned.

The head architect of Gangaikonda temple visited Rudra to endow his blessings. He gifted him with a special seal and gold coins to help him get through various kingdoms. A lot of food was packed for them.

Abhay's wife, Pallavi, and his children were sad and sitting in a corner during the farewell celebration. Abhay was busy hugging all his friends and relatives. He seemed euphoric. Rudra went up to Pallavi and greeted her. She looked disconsolate.

She smiled glumly and said, "Rudra, I am glad you are with him. I have been a miserable wife. I have never been able to give back enough. I don't wish to spoil his happy mood by my harrowing talk. Whenever you can, do tell him I always loved him. Unfortunately, I loved my responsibilities more. He owes us nothing. It's my fault that I lost him."

Rudra was touched by her revelation. What a wonderful woman! Abhay doesn't realize what he is giving up, thought Rudra. He promised Pallavi that he would take care of Abhay and convince him to return. Pallavi gave Rudra a hopeful look.

The celebrations continued well after sunset. A campfire was lit and children played around it, while the elders gossiped. Although other youths of the village chided Rudra for being irresponsible, he knew that they secretly envied him for being able to pursue his dream.

Early at dawn, Rudra and Abhay bade goodbye to their families. Satya hugged Rudra and gave him a bag full of silver, bronze and copper coins.

He said, "Son, do what you are born to do. My blessings shall always be with you. Goodbye."

Rudra walked away from his village with a heavy heart. Pallavi had packed Abhay's favourite food and stuff he would need. Abhay bid her and his children goodbye. The two friends departed leaving their loved ones behind to welcome the new sunrise of their lives.

Three major dynasties – Chandela, Chalukya and Chola – ruled India in the 11th century. The Chalukya kingdom lay between the Chola kingdom, where Rudra lived, and the Chandela kingdom, where he wished to go. The Chalukya kingdom was divided into the Eastern and Western regions, which were ruled by different kings.

The distance between Rudra's village in Tanjore in Dakshinapattam (Chola) and Khajuraho in Jejakabhukti (Chandela) was shorter through the Western Chalukya kingdom. But the Cholas and Western Chalukyas were always at war. Hence, Rudra and Abhay had to take a longer route through the Eastern Chalukya kingdom. The Cholas and Eastern Chalukyas shared friendly ties.

They walked from sunrise to sunset and passed several villages on their way. Whenever empty bullock carts passed, Rudra and Abhay hitchhiked. They learned about various cultures of different villages. They also witnessed the gradual transition of culture, language, cuisine and traditional clothing. There was so much to learn and seek, thought Rudra.

Abhay, on the other hand, spent his time ogling at women from different villages. He was bashed and threatened at several villages for his behaviour, but they always forgave him because of Rudra's intervention.

At night, Rudra and Abhay often took shelter at village temples. The temple priest would guide them to houses that offered food either free or at a minimal price, or in exchange for some labour.

One night after dinner, when Rudra was retiring on a jute cot outside a house that had offered them food, he heard some noise in the house. He went to check and saw Abhay leaning and trying to touch the lady of the house. He jumped through a window to prevent Abhay from committing the act. This awakened the other householders. Rudra was caught and beaten. Abhay did not intervene to own up his doing. Rudra suffered silently to protect his friend and his promise to Pallavi.

After they were banished from the village in the middle of the night, Abhay was guilt-ridden.

He approached Rudra and said, "I am sorry. It's not what you think. I wasn't sneaking up on her without her permission. The young widow had invited me to her bed. I was attracted because of her voluptuous assets. I should have owned up."

A battered Rudra was fuming with rage. "You should have. I only hope that someday you realize what you have left behind."

"I can never pay back all that you do for me, Rudra, not in this lifetime."

"Perhaps in the next," said Rudra and continued nursing his wounds.

They travelled for twenty days, crossed the tributaries of Krishna and Godavari rivers, and finally reached the banks of the Narmada river. The elders of their village in Tanjore had cautioned them about this region. Fierce battles were usually fought between the Cholas and Western Chalukyas on the banks of Narmada.

The sun was down and the riverbank seemed peaceful that day. Rudra lit a fire on a clear area near the bank. The reflection of the moon in the waters of Narmada was mesmerizing. The two friends settled around the fire under the moonlit sky.

Rudra gazed across the river and said, "Jejakabhukti, our destiny, lies just across the Narmada. Tomorrow will be a new beginning. You go to sleep, I'll watch for us tonight."

Abhay saw the glow on Rudra's face and asked, "Rudra, do you never long for a woman? Don't you realize what you are missing? The intimacy and moments of celestial bliss. Ah!"

"I am a man. I have my ways to vent out my longings. Besides, I have always been in love with her."

"Who is her?"

"I don't know. I have to figure that out."

Abhay sighed and said, "So you vent out by meditating, chanting 'Om namah Shivaya', playing with kids, spending time with me and doing excruciating physical labour?"

"Well, that, and there are other things too."

"Meaning?"

"Use your imagination. Go to sleep and dream. And let me and my bliss be."

Abhay glanced at the muscular body and handsome face of his friend and slept wondering about other ways to vent out sexual longings.

At dawn, Rudra awakened Abhay and said, "I am going to fetch a boatman before the soldiers of both kingdoms arrive. You watch for yourself."

Abhay mumbled a sleepy, "Okay," and went back to sleep.

A few moments later, he was rudely awakened by some soldiers. He opened his eyes and saw four soldiers, two each from Chola and Chalukya kingdoms, standing around him. The blades of their swords were close to his neck. Any movement or even heavy breathing would have cut his throat. He moved his eyeballs to look at them.

"Chola or Chalukya?" they kept asking.

He knew that he would lose his life, no matter what he replied.

Rudra was back just in time. He intervened and said, "Chandela."

The soldiers looked at each other and asked, "What is the policy for Chandelas?"

They shrugged their shoulders. One of them asked, "How do we believe you?"

Rudra removed the seal given to him by his head architect.

They looked at the seal and asked, "What is this? And it says Chola."

Rudra replied, "We are Chandelas on a visit to study the art and culture of the Cholas and Chalukyas. We are on our way back."

The soldiers looked unconvinced, "What part of Chandela kingdom are you from?"

Rudra promptly replied, "Khajuraho."

The soldiers looked at each other and began laughing, "We too would like to visit the place for exchange of you know what."

They laughed again. "If you want to live, leave this place immediately. Other soldiers are not as goodhearted as we are."

Rudra and Abhay hurried towards the waiting boatman and asked him to row.

"What is it about Khajuraho? I already owe it my life," said Abhay.

Rudra widened his eyes and asked, "Only to Khajuraho? Well, you are welcome."

Abhay whispered an embarrassed "Thank you," and they were ferried across the river.

After about eight hours, Rudra and Abhay reached Jejakabhukti. They continued their journey to Khajuraho. They travelled on foot for five days while delightfully admiring the culture, dressing, language and scenery of the land. The greenery of Dakshinapattam was replaced by sparsely vegetated mountain ranges of Jejakabhukti.

Jejakabhukti was a hub for mining precious metals and stones and creating stunning artworks. The rich booty of Jejakabhukti had attracted the attention of Mahmud of Ghazni, who had recently re-attacked Chandela kingdom. However, King Vidyadhara's army had put up a brave fight and Mahmud had to retreat.

The general atmosphere was triumphantly joyful. Trade was at its peak. King Vidyadhara declared that they would celebrate their victory by paying homage to Lord Shiva by building a huge and unique temple devoted to him.

Rudra and Abhay were welcomed at most villages. Rudra had warned Abhay against any misbehaviour with women in the foreign kingdom. On the morning of the sixth day of their journey, they saw the most awesome sight – the golden date palm (*khajoor*) trees.

The central areas of the date palm trees shone in the sunlight, giving them a central golden glow. The trees decorated both sides of concrete long roads at the various entrance gates of Khajuraho. These khajoor trees justified the name 'Khajuraho' given to the city.

Stone benches built on either side of the road looked welcoming. Rudra and Abhay sat there for a couple of hours before entering the city. The city had three entrances – western, eastern and southern. Rudra and Abhay were at the western entrance. A huge white-marble sculpture of a woman with folded hands stood at the western entrance. The sight was very appeasing.

Rudra showed the seal he was carrying to the guards at the entrance. Rudra and Abhay were asked to wait in a queue for special artists. There were several other lines. Some of these were for mine labourers, traders, business strategists, tourists from other kingdoms and refugees from war torn areas. The verification process was tedious. Each professional had to undergo tests to prove his proficiency. Mine labourers were put through strenuous physical tests.

Rudra and Abhay acquainted themselves with the artists from other kingdoms. They realized that they were just drops in a huge ocean after meeting several of their kind. Like them, all other artists were also decorated achievers of their kingdoms.

After all the immigrants and visitors were separated into different areas, the head architect and the head sculptor visited the areas. Everyone stood up to honour the two heads. The head sculptor was Master Chiru who was trained by Grandmaster sculptor Sivdutt. The head architect was Master Hosha, who had designed some of the widely known multiple *shikhara* temples of Khajuraho.

Heads of each temple reported to their respective grandmasters, who were supervising the construction of at least eight temples at the same time.

Each of the immigrant sculptors was given a square-shaped sandstone of one square meter and asked to carve something. After about five hours, the head sculptors reviewed the artworks.

Master Chiru saw Rudra's sculpture. He had sculpted a *Shivalinga* and a pair of hands pouring water on it. The details of the hands and depiction of water in the sculpture was stunning. Master Chiru was impressed with Rudra's work. He took an instant liking to Rudra.

Abhay had sculpted an outline of a couple in embrace. Although he had not been able to complete the details, the outlines were very clean, indicating good quality work. Both friends were hired.

A supervisor who managed the hiring process offered them good wages. All selected candidates could choose to work at any of the eight temples. Rudra and Abhay chose the Kandariya Mahadev Temple.

The supervisor directed them to a dormitory closest to the temple. They registered their names at the dormitory and paid deposits.

Next morning, a loud sound of ringing bells awakened them. All of them were shown a place to freshen up and were asked to settle in the temple courtyard for morning yoga and discourse before breakfast.

Respective masters of each temple addressed the artisans and labourers. Master Chiru began with deep breathing exercises for the group.

He addressed them, "All of you are going to work at Kandariya Mahadev Temple. This is going to be the tallest and most magnificent temple ever built in Khajuraho. You may have to work at heights. Some of you may fall and injure yourselves. Some of you may even lose your life. Anyone who wishes to back out or move to another temple may do so right now. The compensation paid for this temple is the highest in view of the risk involved. Passion, and not compensation, should be the criteria to risk your life."

This revelation caused disturbance in the group. Two artisans and three labourers left the premises to work at safer sites. Rudra and Abhay remained firmly seated.

The master continued, "Kandariya Mahadev is the depiction of Lord Shiva in a cave in Mount Kailash. Hence, the temple will have multiple *shikharas* representing his abode in the Himalayas. The main idol in the womb of the temple will be a *Shivalinga*."

Master Chiru and the group chanted 'Om namah Shivaya' several times before continuing, "At Chandela, we have always encouraged freedom of expression of art and culture. That is evident from our sculptures in the older temples. This has defamed us in the eyes of others, but we remain firm. I suggest that before beginning work, you all should visit the Lakshmana and Vishwanath temples to experience what I mean.

"Lord Shiva is a deity who disregards all worldly pleasures. Human life has four goals – *Kama, Arth, Dharma* and *Moksha*. All humans need to follow a certain path to attain the ultimate goal of their lives, which is moksha. Moksha is relief from the cycle of birth and death. Unless we experience and express kama, meaning our desires, physical or mental, we may not be able to overcome it. The other two goals of human life are arth, accumulation of wealth and power, and dharma, performing our duty towards our society and self.

"All of us are in different phases of our lives. Some would be able to achieve all goals in one lifetime, while others may require several lives to attain their goals. Age of a person is no representation of the goal he is set to achieve.

"As artists, we are aware that art is a deep expression of our moods, feelings and beliefs. I want you to reflect and start sculpting your most passionate desires. Don't hold yourself back. I shall ask no questions regarding your sculpture.

"However, I may reject or modify it for quality purposes. For purpose of uniformity in the temple design, the basic geometry of all earthly and divine figures will be same. Any questions?"

Master Chiru looked around for raised hands.

Rudra asked, "Master, where would our sculptures be exhibited?"

Master Chiru replied, "The sculptures depicting kama, arth and dharma would be displayed on the exterior walls of the temple. Only artisans who have overcome these goals of life would be allowed to work in the interior of the temple. I do understand that this would hardly leave any sculptors to work in the interiors; hence, to begin with, I have invited a few sculptors who have worked in the interiors of the older temples.

"Our temple sculptures will depict the souls of sculptors who have created them. Souls in various stages of maturity, souls in various stages of salvation. Devotees visiting these temples need to understand the duties and desires they have to fulfil and overcome to reach the womb of their souls and their final destination of moksha to be one with Lord Shiva."

The group was speechless after attaining this enlightenment. Never before had any of their masters trained their minds before beginning their work. They had always emphasized on achieving perfection in geometry and finesse in their sculptures.

After this session, the artists performed *surya namaskar* and chanted several mantras. After breakfast, they proceeded to visit the other temples. There were at least sixty temples in Khajuraho at that time. It was impossible to see all of them in one day. They visited the most popular ones, which included the Lakshmana and Vishwanath temples.

They were awestruck by the detailing in the sculptures. They were dumbfounded on seeing the bold erotic sculptures. They took blessings of the main deity of each temple before beginning their work. That night, all of them were deeply lost in thoughts of the sculpture they would create the next morning.

The next day, Master Chiru individually tutored each artist. He asked the artists to be ready with an idea of the sculpture they had in mind. The sculptors came up with various ideas such as sculptures depicting a married couple, a family, lovers in embrace, animals, hunting, war scenes, processions of celebrations, etc.

Abhay informed Master Chiru that he wished to complete the sculpture he had started during the test. Rudra couldn't think of anything passionate enough to evoke his interest and said that he wished to sculpt a meditating man.

Master Chiru granted permission to begin work after he explained the general architecture of the temple and the finer geometrical details of the figures they were to sculpt.

This was the first time that the sculptors would create their own ideas. This was their first-hand experience of creative liberty. Rudra realized that it wasn't easy to generate innovative ideas. His respect for his masters and for their dedication to their profession grew manifold. He had always thought that supervising and directing others was much easier than actually doing the job.

Meanwhile, Master Hosha directed his team to begin building a platform for the temple. The team began by digging the premises to lay the foundation stones. The speciality of the temple structure was that no binding material was used to bind the stones together. Special interlocking joints were carved in adjacent stones to hold them together.

Each worker had his weekly day-off on different days. Rudra and Abhay had requested to get an off on the same day of the week. Their request was granted.

Older workers had told Abhay of a special place he could visit to relax on nights before his day-offs. And on his day-offs, he could visit a nearby market to buy his weekly requirements. The supervisor had offered them an advance payment to buy their weekly resources.

He told Rudra, "Tonight, we will visit 'the den' and have some fun."

"What is the den?"

Abhay smiled sheepishly and said, "It is the heaven for all immigrants. It is the reason why people want to work at Khajuraho. At the den, a man narrates paragraphs from the *Kamasutra*, and then, we have a paid option of actually experiencing his stories. This experience will motivate us to create erotic sculptures similar to the ones in Lakshmana and Vishwanath temples."

"You mean the actual *Kamashastra*?"

"Nah, his interpretation and modification."

Rudra informed Abhay that he would skip his invitation as he wasn't feeling too well. Abhay went ahead with the other workers. Rudra spent his day with an old man who was sculpting an image of a father and son.

The old man said, "When I lived with my family, I never realized their value. A few years ago, my entire family was wiped out due to an illness that affected my village. After they were no more, I realized what they meant. I have nowhere to go and no one to earn for. I spend my time carving out my family moments. I have got stuck in time."

Rudra felt sorry for the man and made it a point to spend time chatting with him. Abhay became a regular visitor to the den and splurged all his earnings. He had almost no savings to send home.

He would always tell Rudra, "Next time, definitely."

Rudra would send a part of his earning and messages to both their families. All the neighbouring kingdoms had integrated and set up a service for transporting goods and earnings to promote trade and immigration.

With increasing visits of the artisans to the den, the sculptures became more erotic. Some artisans would return after the *Kamasutra* session and put their imagination to work, whereas others like Abhay would pay exorbitantly to experience their imagination.

The sculptures now included nude nymphs with voluptuous breasts in sensual poses, lovers in intimate positions, copulating couples in various positions, oral sex, anal sex, sex with a horse and one man making love to multiple women.

Abhay was sculpting out a man performing headstand and, at the same time, copulating with a woman sitting on him with support of nude nymphs on either side. The man was fingering the two supporting nymphs. Rudra was shocked to see the image.

He asked, "Have you actually done this or is this your imagination?"

Abhay replied proudly, "I have mastered the art of enjoying sex, but this, my friend, is my imagination and my aspiration. I have performed this act with three women in lying down position. But you are the only one who knows the truth and I trust you to keep my secret."

Rudra was still making figures of goddesses and praying men.

Abhay was the most sought-after artist in the dormitory. He would often coach young men in the art of experiencing ultimate bliss. Rudra was often tempted to visit the den to experience the bliss described by Abhay. He was beginning to lose hope that he would actually meet the woman of his dreams.

The platform of the temple was ready and Master Chiru was selecting and segregating the sculptures to be fixed on various walls of the temple. He was working in coordination with Master Hosha to interlock the stones and have continuity of designs on them.

Rudra went to meet Master Chiru, who was sculpting the main entrance of the temple. He was working on a huge stone and sculpting figures of two crocodiles, one on either side of the temple entrance. He looked at Rudra and acknowledged him.

Rudra greeted him and sat down, "Sir, may I work with you? I seem to have developed an artist's block."

"Hmm," replied Master Chiru. "Sit down son. I hear that Abhay has been coaxing you to visit the den?"

Rudra was uncomfortable at the mention. "Master, is something wrong with me? I don't seem to long what most people seem to enjoy."

Master Chiru smiled. "As I said before, all souls are in different stages of maturity attained over several lifetimes. That's why all of us are different with different aspirations and spiritual goals. You will be twenty-eight soon. Follow your heart."

"Master, don't you have any longings? You always seem to be in control of yourself. No anger, no judgement. Always cool and content."

"As I said before, we all are here to train our souls. Situations don't change, but reactions certainly do."

"Sir, how will I know when I am ready to work in the womb of the temple?"

"Trust me, you will know, son. All of us eventually do. You know that you are not ready now. You are waiting for something, although you are not sure what. When you are ready too, you shall know."

"One last question, Master. Is there something called eternal bliss?"

"Son, no emotion is eternal. The word 'motion' in 'emotion' suggests that it is in constant state of movement. When you are ready, you will know how to detach yourself from these emotions. You will seek to achieve higher goals for yourself and those around you."

Rudra felt the urge to visit the den once. What harm would come from a single visit?

Abhay was overjoyed on learning that Rudra had finally made up his mind to visit the den. The den was located near the forest close to Vishwanath Temple. It was well sequestered in the woods. The entrance of the den had erotic sculptures similar to ones in Vishwanath and Lakshmana temples. Abhay paid for their entry.

Rudra was amazed to see how the twisted minds of some people had managed to lure others and focus only on the erotic aspect of the temple sculptures. They had cunningly left out all the other events that formed almost 90% of the external sculptures.

Rudra was sure that like *Kamasutra*, over a period, the teachings of Khajuraho too were at the risk of being warped and interpreted differently than intended.

Some young men at the entrance of the den were asking the visitors if they were interested in booking a reality experience of any of the sculpted postures or of *Kamasutra* stories. Abhay winked at Rudra and asked if he was interested. Rudra smiled and nodded negatively.

Next to the den were two more entrances. One was marked 'Smoke and Mahua paradise' that served chillum filled with hashish and intoxicating Mahua flower drinks.

The other was 'Gambler's paradise' where most workers splurged their earnings playing a certain 'cowry game'.

The *Kamasutra* narration show was packed. The narrator was a middle-aged handsome man.

He began, "Today, I will tell you a story of a woman who fell in love with her husband's friend. Her husband was a warrior and often visited and stayed on warfronts. The woman was lonely and her husband's friend was aware of that. He felt sorry for her."

The narration was supported by dramatization of the act by male and female actors.

"One day, the friend stalked her. She was alone in her house. Unaware of his presence, she began disrobing in front of a mirror, ornament by ornament, robe by robe, revealing her beautiful body. She stood in front of a mirror and admired herself. 'What a waste of my youth,' she thought to herself. 'Soon, I will lose my youthful body without having enjoyed and experienced the ultimate bliss.' She began touching herself over her breast and between her thighs.

"The friend who was watching her from behind a curtain could no longer control his desire. He felt that he would be obliging his friend and his wife by satisfying her. He decided to sacrifice his morality for them, 'What a noble thought!' he thought.

"When he was unable to control himself, he moved towards his friend's wife. The wife had noticed the friend's movement in the mirror. She too wanted him. She began posing by accentuating her hips, holding and crushing her breasts and caressing her nipples. She walked gracefully and dipped herself into a small water pond in her house. Fragrant rose petals filled the pond. She stood in the pond with her exposed breasts and inviting nipples. A few rose petals entangled in her wet hair and stuck to her wet body looked sensuous.

"The friend began disrobing, exposing his muscular body. He was breathing heavily. He experienced a weird sense of pleasure in acquiring something that was not his. He wanted to feel her smooth and curvaceous body. He wanted to taste and kiss every part of her. He entered the pond. He walked towards her. In no time, he held her, crushed her against his body and had her lips in his mouth.

"Suddenly, the two felt the presence of another person in the pond. The woman's husband had joined them."

Rudra looked around. There was complete silence. Most men were breathing heavily. Some of them had their hands on their groins. He too could feel his manhood growing. He looked at Abhay; he was vigorously stroking his manhood.

The sight of a naked beautiful lady drenched in a pond full of water and rose petals left very little to imagination. Two semi-nude men surrounded her in the water and touched her erotically. The sight was very arousing.

After a while, when the story was over, Abhay looked around. Rudra was nowhere. He must have gone for a reality experience, thought Abhay, smiling.

Rudra had wandered outside the show into the woods. He walked towards Vishwanath Temple. His thoughts went out to Pallavi, Abhay's wife. She was beautiful. What if she was missing Abhay and cheating on him. She had all the right to do so, thought Rudra. Wasn't Abhay doing the same?

He shook his head to drive out the thought of his friend's wife. He hated himself for thinking about Pallavi during the narration. Was he imagining himself in place of the friend's husband?

'No,' he violently shook off the thought. What is wrong with me? These narrations could destroy the very soul of a person, he thought. He was never coming back. He decided to visit Master Chiru the next day to seek permission to begin working in the womb of the temple.

Engrossed in his thoughts, he reached Vishwanath Temple. The temple was lit with oil lamps. People were moving out of the temple after the evening *aarti*. He was relieved to be out of the den.

He was standing in the temple premises when a lady collided with him. She seemed to be in a hurry. Her body and head were covered with a cotton stole. Rudra could see her beautiful face in the dim light of the oil lamps. She was young and had a light brown complexion.

Her kohl-lined brown eyes were filled with fear. A couple of freckles on her smooth forehead looked attractive.

Rudra was so engrossed in admiring her beautiful lips and the black beauty spot on her chin that he did not hear what she was saying.

She shook him and said, "Please help me. Those two thugs want to rob me. They have been following me for a while."

She was nervously biting her lower lip. Rudra looked behind her. Two strong looking men, one bald and the other with a moustache and beard were hurrying towards them.

Rudra led the lady by her elbow and disappeared around the corner. They moved out of a gate at the back of the temple and disappeared into the woods. For some time, they could hear the thugs following them, but soon, there were no noises. The thugs had given up.

Rudra asked the young woman, "Who are you? What do they want to rob?"

The woman removed her stole. Rudra was shocked to see that she was wearing numerous gold and silver jewellery items studded with precious stones that glittered in the night.

"Whoa! Are you from the royal family?" he asked.

"My name is Mohini. The thugs want my jewellery," she replied.

"Those were not thugs. They were royal soldiers. Now give me the truth!"

Mohini covered herself with the stole and turned around to check the surroundings.

She said, "Impressive! You are very smart. I belong to the royal family. So, don't even think of harming me. They have seen you and will hunt you down. I have run away from the palace."

"Why?"

"Because I want to live a normal life. I don't want to spend my days doing my hair and clothes, smiling unnecessarily at strangers and behaving myself."

Rudra was amused by her explanation.

"So, what's your plan?" he asked.

"Plan? Well, I have no plan. You tell me," she replied.

Rudra was shocked. "Me? How am I involved? You eloped on your own. In the morning, you and I go separate ways."

Mohini was angry. "Why wait until morning? I am going right now."

"Very well, be my guest," replied Rudra while preparing a place to lie down and relax.

Mohini turned around to go, but stepped back when she heard howls of wolves. "No. Why should I take orders from you? I will wait until morning."

She removed her stole and spread it before sitting on it. Rudra got up and lit a small fire to keep animals away in case he fell asleep. He was surprised to discover that he was enjoying teasing Mohini. Is she the one? No, I shouldn't get too hopeful, he thought.

"Don't get too hopeful, I am not going to fall asleep. I don't trust you," said Mohini.

"Well, the feeling is mutual," replied Rudra scornfully.

However, Mohini was asleep in no time. Rudra was unable to sleep and admired her all night. At dawn, he saw rays of sunlight glowing through her hair and illuminating her face. The sight was mesmerizing. She moved a little. Rudra looked away and pretended to be asleep. She got up and looked around.

Rudra pretended to get up from sleep and asked, "You are still here? I was hoping you were gone."

"Really? The jungle doesn't belong to you."

She began removing her ornaments and collecting them in her stole.

"Good decision," said Rudra, "before you attract attention of actual thugs. But what about your royal clothes?"

She looked at her heavy clothes and then moved towards Rudra and grabbed his stole that was knotted around his waist. Rudra almost missed a beat on seeing her move animatedly towards him. He was shocked by her action.

He gripped her hand that held his stole and said, "How about asking for something instead of grabbing it? Doesn't requesting suit royal families?"

"Well, you get what you deserve. In your case, it's spite," she replied, freeing her hand from his grip.

"Very well, that makes it easy. I don't have to justify my behaviour."

He got up, stretched his body and began walking.

He noticed that Mohini was following him. He turned around and asked, "Now what? The forest is huge. We walk separate ways."

"Alright." She smirked and turned to go the other way.

Rudra was uneasy after she was out of sight. He began searching for her. He had gone too far this time. How could he leave a woman alone in a forest? What had gotten into him, he thought. He reached the site where they had spent the night. Mohini was sitting there and weeping.

He went towards her and gently said, "You wait here. I'll be back in a moment."

He returned after sometime with a cotton skirt, top and stole. "Here, change into these."

"Where did you find them?"

"Picked them from outside a lonely house in the forest. I left some coins in return."

"Forced trade?" She chuckled.

She went behind a tree and changed. She was evidently relieved after getting rid of the royal attire. She kept talking about the ways of royal families and how annoying she found them. Rudra acted as if he was not interested, but did not miss a word of what she was saying.

Rudra and Mohini finally found their way out of the woods. After walking a short distance, they entered a busy area. The weekly market was in progress. People were selling various items in small and decorated pushcarts.

Mohini was hungry. She gave her gold earring to Rudra and asked him to buy some food.

He was offended by her gesture. "You can keep it. I am capable of feeding you. Besides, I don't want to be labelled as a thug of royal jewellery."

Mohini grimaced and took it back.

Suddenly, many soldiers barged into the market. They were enquiring about something with the local shopkeepers. Rudra saw the two thug soldiers who had been following Mohini the previous night. He asked Mohini to cover her face and protectively pushed her behind him. They moved hiding behind mobs of people.

He wrapped his stole around his face and asked a shopkeeper, "What's with the commotion?"

The shopkeeper replied, "The soldiers are hunting for army chief Veer's runaway bride."

Rudra angrily led Mohini to a secluded alley. "Do you ever speak the truth? Who are you? Are you the runaway bride?"

Mohini was guilt-ridden. "Yes, I am Veer's runaway bride. I took off just minutes before the wedding."

"Why?"

"I didn't lie about my reason of running away. Veer is a decorated army chief with numerous attendants at his service. I am not royal, but after marrying Veer, I would be close to it. I am close friends with the princesses of royal families and hate their lifestyle. Besides, I don't want to be the fifth wife of someone."

"Fifth wife? Is this another bluff?"

"I swear by Goddess Chausath Yogini, this is the truth," replied Mohini batting her eyelashes.

Rudra's heart melted a bit. "Maybe he is a good man. You should return."

"Maybe, but I want my own personal husband and not a visitor after months. I want to cherish and share every moment of my life with someone. Veer may be a great soldier, but I am not interested. Could you get me out of here? Just one last time... please."

She looked so innocent and vulnerable that Rudra did not have the heart to refuse.

"Very well, I have a plan. I work at Kandariya Mahadev. Would you like to come there?"

Mohini was excited. "Yes! I'd love that! We could buy some men's clothing and I could disguise myself."

Rudra glanced at her heavy breasts, scratched his head and said, "Well, that doesn't seem to be a good idea. You may not be able to pull it for long. Why don't you pose as an orphan girl?"

Though unconvinced, she agreed.

Rudra dodged the soldiers and bought all the necessary things from the market. They slipped out unnoticed and walked to Kandariya Mahadev Temple. It was his day off. Abhay was eagerly waiting to hear about Rudra's reality experience after the *Kamasutra* show.

As soon as Rudra entered the temple premises, Abhay confronted him. "Where have you been? Did you spend all your savings at the den? And who is this? I don't think you are allowed to bring women from the den."

Mohini looked at Rudra wide-eyed and echoed the word, "*Den?*"

"No, and no. It's not what you think and not what you think," Rudra said facing each of them one by one. "This is Mohini. I met her at the market. She is a poor orphan. I brought her here to get her a job in the pantry."

Abhay moved closer to Rudra and said with a lopsided smile, "Yeah, right."

Rudra accompanied Mohini to the pantry.

The pot-bellied head cook glanced at Mohini from head to toe and asked, "Have you ever worked before?"

"Er ... no."

"Hmm. But you do know how to cook, right?" he asked.

Mohini looked at Rudra for help.

Rudra interrupted, "She is a fast learner."

The cook looked at Rudra and asked, "How do you know? You just met her. Anyway, I will keep her on a trial."

Mohini was overjoyed and almost hugged Rudra. The cook looked at her disapprovingly. Mohini backed off. Rudra returned to the dormitory.

Abhay was already waiting for him, "Time for the truth, brother."

Rudra narrated the entire incident.

Abhay said, "So you walked out all aroused from the *Kamasutra* narration, met this beautiful woman, spent a night with her and came back a virgin?"

"She is innocent and trusts me."

"Is my brother in love?"

Rudra chuckled. "Don't be silly. She needs help. She needs to be protected."

Rudra's mood was lifted after the incident. He eagerly awaited mealtimes to catch a glimpse of Mohini. She had filled the dull atmosphere of the temple with life. Rudra began sculpting figures of maidens in various poses such as looking into a mirror, applying kohl, knotting their girdle, etc.

Master Chiru complimented Rudra on his work and said, "Looks like you have finally found some inspiration."

After about two weeks, the head cook notified Rudra to visit him.

He said, "Son, this girl, Mohini, she is chaos. She tells never-ending stories. My entire staff is hooked on to her stories. This week we have had incidences of delayed, burnt and uncooked meals. She is spoiling my reputation. You have to find her another place to work."

Rudra was horrified. "Sir, please give her one more chance. Could you let her know that I would like to have a word with her in private?"

The cook sighed and said, "You are wasting your time, son."

Rudra was worried. How could she be so irresponsible? Both of them had completely forgotten that Veer's soldiers were still looking for her. He would never be able to protect her in some other place.

The evening passed. Mohini did not visit Rudra. He was angry. At night, he was tossing in bed when he abruptly opened his eyes. He almost shrieked on seeing Mohini stooping over him with a lamp in her hand.

He got up and whispered, "What do you think you are doing?"

"Cook said you wanted to meet in private," she replied batting her eyelashes.

"This is not what I meant," he said in a hushed but angry tone.

"Okay, I'll go back. You send a clearer message next time," she said turning back.

He gripped her hand and said, "No! Meet me at the front entrance of the temple now, understand?"

"Yes sir," she said saluting with her free hand.

Rudra looked around to check on the others.

"Don't worry. I haven't heard anything," mumbled Abhay with closed eyes.

Rudra saw Mohini near the temple platform. Sounds of crickets filled the night. He rushed towards her and cornered her near the platform wall.

"Are you crazy? I asked you to meet me alone at a lonely place in the middle of night, and you agreed? I could do anything to you," he said moving closer and pinning her against the platform wall.

"I came because *you* called and because I…," she paused.

"I what?" he asked leaning against her and glaring into her eyes.

"I … I trust you."

"Oh, great! So, you would come running to meet anyone you think you can trust. I am just *anyone* now," he yelled.

"I am not sure what you mean, but why did you want to meet?"

Rudra controlled his anger. "The cook wants you to find another job. You are distracting others. I have asked for one last chance. Could you please try? Stop chatting, giggling and wasting time with my colleagues."

"Are you jealous?"

"Don't be silly. Do I look jealous?" he said chuckling unconvincingly.

"You always interrupt and pull me away from your colleagues. You even beat up one of them, I heard."

Rudra looked away trying to hide his embarrassment. "He spoke bad things about you."

"So?"

"So, I couldn't tolerate it," replied Rudra looking away from her.

"Why?" asked Mohini confronting him and moving close to him.

"Because I … I …" struggled Rudra.

"I what?" demanded Mohini.

"Because I brought you here and because you are mine… I mean you are my responsibility. Besides, I am a good man and would do this for any woman."

"Oh! So, I am 'any woman' now," said Mohini narrowing her eyes.

Rudra sighed and returned to the dormitory thinking about their conversation.

"Did you do it?" asked Abhay.

"Shut up," replied Rudra and went to sleep.

The workers at Kandariya Mahadev Temple were excited about the annual cultural festival of Khajuraho. They were going to present an acrobatic show. Every evening after work, they would gather at the temple premises and practice. The atmosphere was festive. Some workers were practicing to play music, some were performing the acrobats and others were supporting the event by making costumes, props, etc.

Mohini and Rudra were able to grab some moments and glimpses of each other during these practice sessions, although both tried to act as if these were accidental.

One such evening, when a practice session was in progress, a group of labourers was leaning hard on an unsupported pillar. The huge pillar began crashing down. Rudra rushed to support the pillar. He reached under the falling pillar, but was fortunately pulled back by Abhay just in time. He acted reflexively without taking time to process that the pillar was too huge for him. The pillar crushed several labourers. Rudra escaped with some bruises on his hands and legs.

Mohini had witnessed the entire incident. She was shaken on seeing how close Rudra was to his death. She visited Rudra at night with a medicine for his wounds.

She looked at him and asked, "How are you doing now?"

He nodded, "Okay."

"You thought of no one else when you rushed there?" she asked.

"Yes, I did think of the workers who would get crushed. Was I supposed to think of anyone else?"

"Of people who depend on you."

"Which people? None of my family members depends on me. Abhay too has a family of his own."

"What about others?" she asked widening her eyes.

"Could you be more specific please?"

"Sure," she said rubbing the medicine harshly into his wounds.

"Ouch," he winced and smiled mischievously rolling his tongue into his cheeks. His wound was bleeding.

"I ... I," she fumbled.

"I what?" asked Rudra.

"I kind of depend on you."

"Well, I was hoping to hear something else," he said pulling his arm away from her.

The atmosphere at Mahadev Temple was bleak after the accident. The practice stopped for several days. Master Chiru and Master Hosha cancelled the permission to practice in the temple premises citing safety reasons. The workers had to do a lot of convincing to regain permission. The process of hiring new workers to fill in the deficit began.

Meanwhile, Mohini's past horrors came back to haunt her. Soldiers had begun identification parades at several temples to identify the runaway bride of Chief Veer. They were showing hand drawn portraits of Mohini to everyone to help identification.

Rudra and Mohini were terrified.

On the night before the identification parade at their temple, they met.

Mohini told Rudra, "It's time to part. I am going away tonight. I'd rather die than be gifted to Veer. I feel this more strongly now than ever."

"Could you elabourate on the last line?" asked Rudra.

"No, I couldn't," she replied angrily.

"So, what's the plan?" he asked.

"Plan? I have no plan."

"Okay, meet me at the temple gate after everybody is down. Get all your belongings and enough food for both of us."

"Us? I couldn't put you in danger. It's not going to be fun anymore."

"I know. That's why, I have to be with you."

At the dormitory, he spoke to Abhay, "Brother, I am going away tonight with Mohini. I have to keep her safe. I will spend some time in the forest near Vishwanath Temple and then move to some remote village when it is safe. After a few months, I will try to go back to Dakshinapattam. I am going to miss you."

Abhay was devastated.

He hugged Rudra, "I will accompany you just like Lakshman accompanied Ram."

"No, you stay here and watch for me. Besides, I have promised Pallavi that I will keep you safe."

Abhay helped him pack and gave him some gold coins, "You will need these."

After everybody was asleep, Rudra slipped out of the dormitory with his belongings. Mohini was already at the gate.

They walked all night and passed a few sleeping villages and a few temples of the eastern group. Mohini wanted to visit the temples, but Rudra refused to avoid raising suspicion and leaving trails of their whereabouts. At dawn, they halted in a village. They posed as a couple and rested for some time.

Luckily, a bullock cart owner, who was on his way to a village outside the forest near River Ken, offered them a ride. Late at night, they were dropped outside the forest. Rudra had changed his original plan of hiding in the forest close to Vishwanath Temple. However, he was unable to inform Abhay of his change in plan.

Rudra lighted a fire outside the forest. He asked Mohini to sleep while he kept a watch. It would be best to enter the forest at daytime, he thought.

At dawn, he awakened Mohini and together they entered the forest. They passed through dense thicket of trees for some distance. After some distance, surprisingly, the forest had numerous clear areas.

"What if we would have confided in Master Chiru and Master Hosha? Would they have helped us?" asked Mohini.

"Maybe. But that would mean too many mouths would have to keep shut. Anybody could have taken advantage of our situation. I didn't want to risk losing you."

"Why?" asked Mohini smiling mischievously.

"Because I ... I...."

"I what?" asked Mohini blocking his way.

"Because I would miss your silly chattering, stupid questioning, eyelid fluttering and lip biting."

After walking for some more distance, they reached a clear lake. They decided to rest there for some time. Rudra took a nap while Mohini kept a watch. She got a chance to look closely at the man she had fallen in love with. She relived all the moments she had spent with him since the time they met. The more she thought, the more she fell in love with him. He had never let her down. So trustworthy, she thought. She moved her hands on his face, lips, chest and muscular arms. She slept next to him for a while and felt the warmth of his body.

Before proceeding, Rudra wanted to take a dip in the lake. He undressed and entered the lake. He swam in the lake, emitting masculinity from every part and movement of his body. Mohini hid his clothes and dared him to come out. He asked her to give him a hand and pulled her into the water with him. She got soaked in the cold water and began shivering.

Rudra felt sorry and moved closer to provide her warmth. Glistening water droplets were dripping from his hair and the thick silver earring he wore in his right ear. His muscular chest was mildly covered with matted hair.

"You are good, you know," she said shivering.

He chuckled and replied, "You are not so bad either."

He carried her out of the water. Her clothes stuck to her, revealing parts of her body.

He put her down and helped her dry her body. Her heart was beating fast. She had butterflies in her stomach every time his hands touched her skin to wipe her dry. He knew the effect he had on her and enjoyed teasing her with intentional sensual touches on her bare back and stomach. She wanted these moments to last forever.

Rudra controlled himself with great difficulty. He asked her to change and they moved from the spot. It was late afternoon when they heard a distant voice.

"Help... help."

"Did you hear that?" asked Rudra.

"Yeah. There is someone else in this forest, a woman."

"Let's hurry."

On reaching the site, they saw a woman standing next to a man convulsing on the ground. Rudra rushed to the man.

"A black cobra has bitten him. Please save him," the woman pleaded.

"How?" asked Rudra.

"Help me carry him to my village. The elders in the village have a concoction that will save him."

Rudra carried the man on his shoulders and ran as fast as he could. In a few minutes, they reached a village in the forest, the village of forest miners. The villagers administered the unconscious man some potion. The woman thanked Rudra for his timely help. She provided them with food and a place to stay.

Next day, the man felt better. He and his wife visited Rudra and Mohini.

"How are you feeling?" asked Rudra.

"My wife told me how you helped us. I am grateful," he said with folded hands.

"It was nothing," replied Rudra.

"My name is Aamir," said the man.

"Aamir?" questioned Rudra. "That is a... a... different name."

"I know what you are thinking. I was a soldier with the army of Mahmud of Ghazni. I fell in love with Shamli and stayed back in this country. There are many like me in this village. This is a beautiful country, but we have never dared to cross the limits of this forest fearing King Vidyadhara's wrath."

Rudra and Mohini took a while to digest the story. They looked uneasy.

"Don't worry, you are safe here," reassured Aamir. "Tell me your story."

Rudra narrated his story.

"We are both victims of love," joked Aamir.

Aamir told Rudra that he could live in the village as long as he liked. They became good friends. Rudra worked with the village men and helped in hunting and mining. Some men would go to the forest boundary and exchange their resources for goods that the passing bullock carts brought from nearby villages. Rudra never went outside the forest.

One day, he told Aamir, "You can go to Kandariya Mahadev Temple and work there. You can meet my friend Abhay. He will help you out. You will have to adopt another name though."

Aamir was delighted. He had always wanted to move out of the forest. Now, he had a chance. Rudra and Mohini were low-spirited after Aamir and Shamli left.

Staying together and controlling their passion for each other was becoming extremely difficult for Rudra and Mohini. Days were easier to pass, but nights were testing. Mohini would often accompany Rudra to the forest.

"I was wondering if you visited the den often," asked Mohini.

"Ah, the den! How do you know about the den?" asked Rudra.

"Everyone in Khajuraho knows about it. It is an open secret. You didn't answer my question?"

"Well yes. Very often."

Mohini asked with a hint of anger in her tone, "Why?"

"Because Khajuraho is a land of immigrant men and men have needs. It is an open secret."

She was quiet for a while. Then, she began to mutter angry curses. He was amused to watch her. He watched her nose flare in anger.

"You said something?" he asked.

"I thought you were different," she shot back.

"Different? In what sense?"

"I thought you see more in a woman than her body."

"I do, but I can't close my eyes to a beautiful woman."

"How many times have you visited? How many women did you... you know... whatever? What did you enjoy the most?"

"So many questions? Are you jealous?"

"Do I look jealous?" she asked angrily.

He tried to remain cool. "Nah. You look just fine."

"So, you don't find me attractive?"

"I never said so."

"Then why haven't you touched me or tried to get close to me?"

He wiped the sweat on her forehead, put her scattered hair strands behind her ear, relieved her lower lip from her bite and replied, "Because I... I..."

"I what?"

"Because I am a good man and would never take advantage of a woman in my shelter."

She stamped his foot and moved ahead.

"Ouch! That hurt," he said hopping on one leg.

They walked without talking for some time. Then he said, "If it is any consolation, the day I met you was my first visit to the den. I walked out without visiting any woman. You can confirm it with Abhay."

She stopped and looked relieved.

A week passed. The villagers had warmly and whole heartedly accepted Rudra and Mohini.

"You never talk about your family. Don't you fear that Veer would harm them because you have run away?" asked Rudra.

"He would, if they were alive," replied Mohini grimly. "My father was a senior army chief. He died in a battle with Mahmud of Ghazni. Veer was a frequent visitor to my house. He would often visit to seek advice from my father. He had proposed marriage several times, but I always refused. My parents never forced me. They wanted me to be happy. After my father's death, my mother was heartbroken and passed away. Veer knew I had no one to fall back on. He announced that he would marry me. His act was looked upon as a great favour. No one bothered to ask my will. So, I ran away just minutes before the wedding. I have never been more proud of myself than on that day. I wish I could personally witness the embarrassment on Veer's face."

Rudra held her hand and said, "I am sorry about your family."

She smiled sadly.

"I was thinking about the sculptures at the temple," she said.

"What about them?"

"They are made from men's point of view about women, life, marriage, love, sex, family, dharma, kama, moksha, etc. Did it never occur to any of you to consider our views? I wish there was a temple with women artisans. Then, we could express ourselves too."

64

"Alright, so why not I build one for you." suggested Rudra impressed by Mohini's views. "I'll help you sculpt the images you have in mind."

"You are not serious."

"I sure am," he said pulling her to a nearby cave. "Look, this could be our temple and we could start right away."

He gathered huge stones from nearby areas and levelled them to prepare to make sculptures. Mohini was happy to see his excitement. She helped him and tried to learn the art. She injured her hands a couple of times and Rudra nursed her wounds. Together, they made sculptures of a man and woman hunting together, a man carrying his lover in his arms, a couple praying together, a warrior woman, marriage, family, etc.

Rudra was happy that Mohini had found a way to express her feelings. Soon, she was capable of working independently. She carved out several sculptures on the walls of the cave too. One day, she sculpted a figure of a woman dressed erotically to impress her lover, and then decided to put it to practice.

In the middle of a cold night, Mohini was trying to awaken Rudra by lovingly whispering his name. He opened his eyes and glanced at Mohini's bed on the floor. She was not there. He got up with a start and looked around in the dark.

A corner of the room was dimly illuminated by a flickering oil lamp and Mohini was standing wearing a few gold ornaments and bare minimum clothes. She was standing in one of the poses sculpted by Rudra at the Mahadev Temple.

Rudra stared at her with wide eyes. He was breathing fast. She gracefully changed poses while looking at him seductively. He tried to look away, but only for a few seconds. Her round firm breasts and erect nipples were moving with the heaving of her chest. Her perfect hips were visible through the transparent shimmering cloth around her waist.

Unable to control himself, he walked towards her. She was breathless on seeing him moving towards her like an animal. He grabbed her and pressed her close to his body. She could feel his warm breath on her forehead. Through his bare chest, she could hear his heartbeats. It sounded like the galloping of horses. She could feel his hard manhood pressed against her body.

"What do you think you are doing?" he whispered.

"Just checking," she replied.

"Checking what?"

"If I am able to arouse you. I was beginning to lose confidence in myself."

"You need more proof?" he asked squashing her even more tightly.

She snuggled and replied, "No."

He broke the embrace and looked at her face closely. He moved close to kiss her. He lightly brushed his lips against hers and walked away. She was aghast. He left her high and dry. Why? She thought to herself. She was not going to back off, not after coming so close. He had gone out of the house.

She draped a bed sheet and followed him out. He was splashing cold water on his face from a canister outside the house. He then picked up his axe and began chopping logs of woods in the courtyard, each stroke stronger than the previous one. Mohini confronted him, while he tried to face away.

"What's wrong?" she whispered hugging him from behind.

"Why are you so persistent? You are unleashing the animal within me. I may not be able to control after a certain point."

"What is holding you back?"

"I want this to be special."

"Oh! You had something else in mind? We could do it your way."

"No, I wanted us to be married," he said, his eyes blazing with desire.

"Okay. So, let us get married now."

"I want us to be married in Dakshinapattam with the blessings of my parents."

"When would that be? What if we can never make it to Dakshinapattam? Besides, we are married in the eyes of the villagers," she tried to persuade him.

"If we are unable to leave this place in a week, we will get married on the coming full moon night," he promised.

"One week!" she shouted rolling her eyes and went to the canister and splashed cold water on her face. "I hope this works, and yes, promise that you won't sleep bare chested for the entire week or I will be unable to control the animal within me," she said looking at him with flaming eyes.

He smiled and said, "I promise."

At Kandariya Mahadev Temple, the disappearance of Rudra and Mohini was the top gossip. Though Abhay claimed ignorance about Rudra's whereabouts, no one believed him. Master Chiru was flustered that Rudra had not confided in him.

Preparation of the acrobatic item for the Khajuraho annual cultural festival had faced a new roadblock. They had to find a replacement for Rudra. Although Abhay too wished to opt out, he was not allowed because the festival was just a week away, on the coming full moon eve. He missed Rudra terribly.

Aamir reached Kandariya Mahadev Temple. News of Rudra and Mohini's safety brought peace to Abhay's mind. He introduced Aamir as Raghu. Raghu was instantly employed as a labourer to fill in for those who had lost their lives in the accident. Abhay and Aamir often chatted about Rudra and Mohini. Although they were careful, news about Rudra and Mohini's whereabouts leaked.

One of the workers decided to use the news to his advantage. He revealed Rudra and Mohini's hiding place to Veer's soldiers. Veer was elated on hearing the news and rewarded the labourer.

The Khajuraho cultural festival was just a couple of days away and Veer was supervising the security of the city and the king. Hence, he was unable to leave immediately to pursue his vengeance. He sent four of his soldiers to capture Rudra and Mohini. Abhay and Aamir were unaware of this new development. They were busy working and putting together the acrobatic show.

The Khajuraho annual cultural festival was the biggest event of Chandela kingdom. It was held in a huge clear area at the base of Vindhya mountain ranges. Huge stone benches were placed around the performance area for people to sit. One side of the area was reserved for the king and the royal family with their personal soldiers and staff. Commoners were seated on the opposite end. The security of the king and city was overseen by Veer.

The place was decorated with fresh flowers of various colours. All the participants were given separate tents near the performance area. The performances included singing, dancing, drama, acrobatics, etc. The most awaited event was a show by a hunting tribe. Every year, the tribe performed a colourful act dramatizing the capture of various wild animals.

In their tent, Abhay and Aamir learnt that Veer had sent soldiers to capture Rudra and Mohini. They wanted to leave immediately to help them. Hence, they went to seek permission from Master Chiru. However, Master Chiru asked them to wait until the event was over to avoid raising suspicion. Master Chiru said that he would arrange horses for Abhay and Aamir in the meantime.

The show began. The excitement in the crowd was palpable. There was a loud applause after every event. Villagers cheered their teams. The king had declared heavy rewards for the winning team. The acrobatic show of the temple workers included daredevil life-threatening stunts. It was an immediate hit.

As soon as the last performance began, Abhay and Aamir left the place on horsebacks. The hunting tribe began its show. This year, they dramatized the hunting of a tiger and a tigress. They began beating drums to corner the wild animals enacted by the tribesmen. The fighting sequence between the hunters and the animal couple was amazingly dramatized.

At the miner's village, Rudra and Mohini were excited about the midnight wedding they had privately organized. They had arranged for a priest to get them married at their cave.

On several occasions during the week, they had tried to escape to Dakshinapattam. However, things were never favourable. In the cave, Rudra and Mohini, dressed as groom and bride, awaited the priest they had invited to get them married.

"Finally, it's time. Tonight, we will commit to be together forever. Any second thoughts?" Rudra asked Mohini.

She shook her head.

"Think about it. I may pursue you in other lifetimes too," he smiled and warned her.

"I'd like that," she replied blushing.

The soldiers sent by Veer to capture Rudra and Mohini had reached the miner's village in the forest. They were enquiring about Rudra and Mohini. At first, the villagers tried to protect the two, but soon gave in to the cruel torture by the soldiers. One of the villagers came to the cave to warn Rudra and Mohini. Both of them quickly fled to the forest to hide from the soldiers.

The soldiers chased them. Rudra and Mohini returned to hide in their cave. Both of them were tired and panting. After some time, they thought that they had managed to trick the soldiers.

"What do you think? Are they gone?" asked Mohini.

"I don't have a good feeling about this. I don't think they will leave soon," replied Rudra. "Let us stay put for a while and escape later in the night," he continued.

"Just when we were about to get married," she sighed looking at her bridal attire.

Rudra gently cupped her face and looked into her eyes and said, "You look beautiful."

They stayed in the cave until dark and moved out when they thought it was safe. They were moving slowly hiding behind trees. The soldiers were not visible. Just then, a soldier pounced on them from a tree. He hit Rudra on his head with a stone. Rudra collapsed, his head bleeding profusely. He could recognize the bald and the bearded thug soldiers from the group of four. Mohini rushed to Rudra's aid, but was captured. She tried to free herself in vain. She was sobbing relentlessly because she thought that Rudra was dead. Soon, she too was unconscious.

At the festival, the hunting tribe had injured the tiger. The tigress tried to fight back, but was captured by the tribesmen. The drama ended with the victory of the hunters. The animal dummies were hung upside down on bamboo sticks. The crowd applauded and the annual show ended on a high note.

It was time for King Vidyadhara's address to his subjects. The king rose and the crowd cheered. He spoke about the great show and announced new policies for the welfare of his kingdom. He announced the winner. The acrobatic show had won the prize. The team collected the reward. No one noticed that Abhay and Aamir were missing from the team.

After the festival, Veer arranged for the safe return of King Vidyadhara. He gave final dispersal instructions to his soldiers. After everything was under control, he, along with six soldiers, rode off to avenge Mohini. Abhay and Aamir knew that Veer would start as soon as the show was over. They avoided taking any unnecessary stopovers to gain time to help Rudra before Veer's arrival.

Mohini gained consciousness after some time. She saw Rudra lying at a little distance. In the moonlight, she could see that he was still bleeding. She looked around; no soldiers seemed to be there. She got up and tried to reach Rudra, but felt a sharp tug in her right leg. They had chained her right ankle to a huge tree trunk outside the cave. She strained to see in the dark and noticed that Rudra's ankle too was chained around another tree on the opposite side.

She called out his name. Rudra did not move. She looked at him helplessly with tear-filled eyes and called out again.

Suddenly, she felt sharp pain on her back. One of the soldiers was whiplashing her. She shrieked in pain. Her cries seemed to stir Rudra. He saw her kneeling before him, crying, her tear drops disappearing into the mud. He saw a soldier lashing out at Mohini. He tried to get up to protect her, but couldn't. The chain restricted him from moving. He was barely able to touch her silhouette.

In spite of the pain, she was overjoyed to see that Rudra was alive. He tried to reach her, but another soldier began whiplashing Rudra too. Both of them collapsed and were unconscious again.

One of the soldiers was mild hearted. He offered water to both of them after the others had gone off to sleep. He explained that he could not release them because he feared Veer. He also warned them that Veer would be visiting soon.

Mohini was resting against the tree. "I am sorry I brought this upon you. I wish we had never met. I never wanted this for you," she said in a soft voice.

"I cherish the day I met you. You gave purpose to my life. I've loved every moment of my life after I met you. I'd do it again without any doubt," Rudra replied gazing, his eyes brimming with love.

She crawled slowly to reach out to him. He held out his hands. They could barely touch each other's fingers.

She sat down frustrated and said, "I had hoped that we would go together to visit your parents after our wedding. We would live happily, have children and grow old together."

"I'll get you out of this. Don't worry. We will find a way. And then, we will visit my village together. There are so many things I want to show you," replied Rudra to cheer Mohini up.

Although she knew they would never get out of this trap, she smiled with tears in her eyes.

Throughout the day, Rudra and Mohini drifted in and out of consciousness. In the evening, one of the soldiers saw that Mohini was trying to crawl towards Rudra again. He hit Mohini on her back with the butt of his whiplash. Mohini was badly hurt and began bleeding from her mouth. Rudra tugged at his already sore and bleeding ankle to free himself. He thumped and clawed the ground in helplessness and frustration.

Mohini looked at him with tears rolling down her eyes and feebly said, "Rudra, the pain is unbearable. You have to let me go. If there is another lifetime, promise me that you will pursue me."

"I will, I promise, but hold on for some more time for my sake."

"How will you remember me in our next lifetime?"

"I don't know. The universe owes us this and will find a way."

Rudra and Mohini were bleeding due to the whiplash injuries.

Abhay and Aamir managed to reach the miner's village. They learnt about Rudra and Mohini's plight from the villagers.

They requested the villagers to help them save Rudra and Mohini. However, the villagers were scared of Veer's wrath. They didn't want the Chandela soldiers to learn that they were enemies left behind from the army of Mahmud of Ghazni.

Abhay and Aamir made up their minds to fight the soldiers on their own. Aamir was a warrior, but Abhay was an artist with no experience of fighting. They knew that they had to hurry because Veer would soon follow them.

They waited for nightfall. Until dark, they hid in bushes near the cave. When they were hiding in the bushes, Abhay noticed that a black cobra was about to bite Aamir. Abhay used a stick and frightened the snake away. Aamir wondered why a cobra wanted to take his life for the second time.

After dark, the soldiers went into the cave and slept. Abhay and Aamir entered the cave and attacked the soldiers. They killed two of them. The good soldier was among the dead.

Shrieks of the dying soldiers alerted the other two soldiers. They held their swords and moved swiftly to attack Abhay and Aamir. The fighting continued outside the cave. The commotion stirred Rudra and Mohini. They were overjoyed to see that Abhay and Aamir had come to their rescue.

One of the soldiers took out a bunch of keys, showed it to Abhay and threw it far into the bushes. Aamir was a very skilled warrior; he managed to defeat and kill the remaining two soldiers.

Abhay approached Rudra and hugged him. He was devastated to see his friend tied up like an animal and bleeding profusely from all over his body. He told Aamir to try cutting the chain with his sword while he went and searched for the keys.

The chain was very thick. Aamir struck it several times using huge stones. After a long time, Aamir was able to free Rudra. Rudra limped towards Mohini. She was lying unconscious. He supported and hugged her. She wiggled a bit. She opened her eyes and smiled on seeing Rudra.

"I told you I will get you out of this." He stroked her ashen face.

"I trusted you. I always have and always will," she managed to whisper.

Just then, Abhay came hurrying. "I can hear a lot of horsemen riding towards us. I think Veer and his soldiers have arrived. I could not find the keys," he said looking frightened, his clothes and face tainted with splattered blood.

He was glad to see that Rudra was free. He and Aamir began striking Mohini's chain. The noise of the moving army was getting louder. Rudra realized that they would not be able to break the chain before the army arrived.

Rudra looked at his friends and urged, "Friends, it's time that you go back. Save yourself. I don't want you both to lose your lives."

"We are not going back without you. We will stay and fight Veer and his army," Aamir replied.

"You know you are no match to Veer and his army, so back off, now," commanded Rudra.

"You have to come with us," said Abhay trying to drag Rudra along.

Rudra pushed him away and said, "I can't leave her."

Mohini tried to stand leaning on Rudra and said, "Your friends are right. You have to go now, for my sake."

"I am not leaving you. Not now, not ever."

He looked at Abhay and signalled him to go. Aamir dragged Abhay and they hid in nearby bushes from where they could still watch Rudra and Mohini.

Rudra looked into Mohini's eyes. They forgot about the pain. He held her with his arms possessively wrapped around her to support her. She stood closely snugged to Rudra's body. Rudra leaned forward and kissed her forehead.

"I think it is time," he said, gently stroking her face.

"I know," she replied, nervously biting her lower lip.

"Are you scared?" he asked while gently relieving her lip from her bite.

"Not as long as you are with me. And you?" she asked blinking her tear-filled eyes.

He nodded negatively and hugged her tightly.

Abhay and Aamir watched the two embrace each other against the backdrop of the full moon. Rudra and Mohini were so engrossed in each other that they did not realize that Veer and his army had reached.

Veer was enraged to see the two locked in an embrace, their final embrace. He picked up a whiplash and lashed the two. However, neither of the two winced. They were lost in each other, unaware of any pain. Burning with anger, Veer picked up a spear and thrust Rudra in his back. The same spear punctured Mohini's chest.

Abhay wanted to scream and rush to Rudra's aid, but was forcibly held back by Aamir. Abhay saw that even in death, Rudra firmly supported Mohini.

'The eternal embrace, orgasm of the souls in love,' he thought to himself. Rudra and Mohini collapsed together, embracing and gazing into each other's eyes. They breathed their last holding each other's image in their souls forever.

Abhay and Aamir wept in the bushes. Veer's soldiers saw the dead bodies of the other soldiers. Veer threatened his soldiers against revealing that their colleagues had died fighting *his* personal battle. They ransacked the cave and buried the dead soldiers outside.

After Veer and his soldiers left, Abhay and Aamir emerged from the bushes. They rushed towards Rudra and Mohini. Their bodies were lying still, holding hands and gazing at each other with eternal bliss on their faces.

Suddenly, Abhay heard a loud noise. He looked up with tearful eyes. Aamir had picked up a huge stone and was trying to break Mohini's chain. Abhay picked up another stone and helped Aamir. After prolonged efforts, the chain gave way. Abhay and Aamir dug the floor of the cave and buried Rudra and Mohini. They placed the sculpture of a man carrying his lover in his arms over the tomb.

Both of them left the forest with heavy hearts. They rode back silently, lost in thoughts.

Abhay was astounded by Rudra's capacity to love someone more that his own life. Rudra had a chance to save himself, but he willingly chose death just to be with Mohini. Was the 'eternal bliss' that Abhay experienced in physical love in the den real? Or, was the 'eternal bliss' that Rudra experienced in selfless love real?

Abhay had never felt such love for anyone, not even for his wife and children. Maybe he was in love with one of the women from the den. He was going to find out.

Aamir was shocked with the uncertainty of life. He just wanted to be with Shamli and hold her forever. He began riding faster.

Meanwhile, Abhay felt shallow for not being able to love anybody more than himself. Did love mean protecting someone? Did it mean providing and caring for someone? Did it mean depending on or trusting someone? No, it must mean getting intellectually, spiritually, emotionally, or physically intimate with someone.

Rudra had always been the protective kind. He was attracted to Mohini and found his purpose in her. So, I guess love has a different meaning to different people, thought Abhay. I have to find out what love means to me. Abhay too began riding faster to match Aamir's pace.

Both of them thought of the times they had spent with Rudra and Mohini. Abhay was Rudra's best friend. He had too many memories. Tears rolled down with each memorable moment that he remembered.

After a couple of days, Abhay and Aamir reached Kandariya Mahadev Temple. They met Master Chiru and narrated the incident. Master Chiru felt sorry for Rudra and Mohini. He informed them that Veer had misinformed everyone that his soldiers had died in a battle with enemy intruders in the forest.

Master Chiru warned Abhay and Aamir, "Veer's ego is still very hurt. He hasn't calmed down even after killing Mohini. He is trying to hunt down Rudra's friends too. It is dangerous for you two to work here. I have spoken to the head engineer of the Jain temple in the east. You two can hide there for some time until this is over. Remember to keep a low profile."

The two of them hid in Master Chiru's quarters and decided to go to the Jain temple at night. Aamir rushed to his quarters to meet Shamli. Abhay made up his mind to visit the den for the last time.

This was Abhay's first daylight visit to the den. It looked different during the day. He met the head lady of the den and asked her if he could meet the woman he was seeing every night. She nodded. Almost fifteen women lined up. Abhay looked at them in shock.

"These are the women you have been sleeping with during the night visits. There are a few more, but they didn't care to come out. Whom do you want to see?"

Abhay looked at each of the women. He did not recognize any of them. Actually, he was unaware that he was sleeping with so many different women. He looked confused.

The head lady tried to help. "Perhaps, you remember her name or her voice?"

He tried to think. He had never cared to ask any of their names or talk to any of them. All he had cared for was his pleasure. He had used them to derive erotic thrill.

"Just close your eyes and think of something that will help you identify the one you are looking for," said the head lady.

Abhay closed his eyes and thought. All he could visualize was Pallavi, caring for him, making love to him, pleasing him, hugging him, being there with him always. He opened his eyes in shock. What a fool he had been! All throughout, he had always been in love with Pallavi. He had carried her along in all his thoughts and acts, but had never taken the time to analyze his feelings for her. He took her for granted because she had always been there for him. He instantly began missing her terribly. He wanted to rush back to her and left the den in a hurry.

At Master Chiru's quarters, Aamir was already waiting for him. "I have decided to go back to the forest with Shamli. From there, I will go back to my country with her. I will leave tonight," he informed Abhay.

Abhay held Aamir's shoulder and said, "I am glad about your decision. I don't want to lose one more friend. I am going to miss you. You be careful of the black cobra in the forest. I am going back to Dakshinapattam after a few days when I can cross the border. For now, I am going to the Jain temple."

That night, Abhay went to the Jain temple. Abhay informed the head engineer that he wanted to go back home. The head engineer said that he understood his plight and pleaded him to work until Veer's unrest had settled. Abhay worked alone. He did not mingle with anyone. He wanted to be left alone. All he could think of was Pallavi.

He was unable to get the image of Rudra and Mohini's last embrace out of his mind. He decided to immortalize 'the eternal embrace'. He began sculpting a figure of a man and woman in an intimate embrace, the man bending a little forward and supporting his lover behind her upper back and waist. After the figures were carved, he began carving a thick metallic chain binding the woman's ankle. The head engineer stopped Abhay from doing that. He warned that someone would get a clue and report it to Veer.

After about another week, the head engineer permitted Abhay to leave for Dakshinapattam. Abhay walked back remembering the moments when Rudra was so excited about coming to Jejakabhukti.

Rudra always felt that Khajuraho was his calling. Indeed! It was. It called him forever!

On reaching his village after almost a month, Abhay decided to visit Rudra's house before visiting his own. He felt relieved and overwhelmed on seeing his village and its people. Everyone seemed to stare at Abhay while he walked towards Rudra's house. It made him uncomfortable. Did they already know about Rudra's death?

At Rudra's house, Rudra's brother welcomed Abhay. Abhay asked for Rudra's parents.

"After you and Rudra left, an epidemic in our village killed many people, especially the elderly and children. We lost our parents to the illness. We did not wish to upset Rudra, so we did not send across the message through the men who delivered his wages," said Rudra's brother.

In a way, Abhay was relieved. It would have been difficult to inform Rudra's parents of his death. Abhay informed Rudra's brother. The house was filled with gloom. The kids were very sad at the loss of their favourite uncle. After some time, Abhay got up to go to his house. Although sad, he was excited to meet Pallavi and his kids. He got up to take leave from Rudra's brother.

"Where are you going?" asked Rudra's brother.

"Home," replied Abhay promptly.

"Don't you know?"

"What?" asked Abhay getting worried and impatient.

"The epidemic, well, it took away your children."

"No!" said Abhay sinking back into the chair.

Rudra's brother gave him a glass of water. Abhay wept like a child. He realized his love for his children only after losing them. He remembered their innocent smiles, pranks and their last goodbyes when he was leaving. He never cared about them. Now, when he wanted to, they were no more. He wanted to rush to Pallavi to comfort her.

"There's more," said Rudra's brother.

Abhay looked at him scared about what was coming.

"After your kids passed away, Pallavi was alone. She wanted to come to Khajuraho to be with you. She always enquired about your wellbeing from the messenger who brought your earnings. The messenger would always say that you were fine."

Abhay was surprised. "But I never sent anything. Oh, Rudra! You provided for my family too."

"Yes. When Pallavi insisted on accompanying the messenger to Khajuraho, he revealed the truth. He told her that you had never ever bothered to enquire about her, and the goods and wages were sent by Rudra. She was dejected on learning the truth. He told her that you splurged your earning in the den. Her children were gone and you didn't care about her. She saw no purpose in living. So, she went up the village hill and jumped. The villagers found her body and performed her last rites. There is no one waiting for you at your house, Abhay. Perhaps, you must return to Khajuraho."

"There is no one waiting for me there too," muttered Abhay and walked out disoriented.

He wandered in the village, trying to find courage to visit his house. He wanted to visit his house to feel the presence of Pallavi. He went home. Huge spider webs were all over his house. Each corner reminded him of Pallavi and his children. All his things were stored neatly, as though Pallavi was anticipating his return.

In a corner of the house, he found messages sent by Rudra on his behalf. He wept bitterly. Khajuraho had given him realization, but ironically, taken away the means to practice it.

He noticed that Pallavi had scribbled a message for Rudra. She wrote that she was indebted to him for providing for her and her children and owed him her life. She did not even think Abhay was worthy of a message. She had lost faith in him. He couldn't think clearly anymore. His brain seemed to have blocked all thoughts.

At dawn, he walked the path taken by Pallavi to the hilltop. He stood at the edge of the hill and looked down. He saw Pallavi smiling and waving.

At last, he had found her. He was never going to leave her. At last, he felt more love for someone than himself. At last, he understood Rudra's death. He smiled and dived to meet Pallavi. As he went down, he could see Pallavi more clearly. He was going to be with her forever.

Shiv got up from his sleep, startled. He was sweating profusely. He was breathless and disoriented. He looked around. He could see daylight outside the hotel balcony. His cell phone was ringing. Someone was knocking on the door. He had dreamt an entire lifetime. A result of learning too much about Khajuraho, he thought. Or, was it an effort by the universe to send him a message? No, that is a silly thought! I don't believe in reincarnation.

Shiv answered the cellphone and opened the door simultaneously. It was Arjun on the phone, "Where have you been, dude?"

"I was sleeping," replied Shiv.

Tony was at the door. He looked visibly worried.

"Did you drug yourself to sleep?" asked Arjun raising his voice.

"I'll call you back," said Shiv and disconnected the phone.

His phone showed thirty-two missed calls from Saloni, fourteen from Mr Sanyal and twenty-six from Arjun. Several unread messages were also popping up on Shiv's cell phone screen.

Shiv looked at Tony standing at the door. He was wearing gumboots and impatiently moving from one leg to another, "Shiv sir, you were to meet me at 9.00 a.m. in the lobby. I was worried. The hotel guys said that you hung a 'Do not disturb' sign on your doorknob and hence, did not let me wake you up. I sneaked my way up here. Are you okay?"

"Tony, I am sorry. Come on in."

He called back Arjun, "Hi! I don't know what happened, but I have been sleeping."

"I was worried."

"Can you let Saloni know that I am fine? I have a number of missed calls from her."

"Oh! Do you want to talk to her? She is here because she didn't know who else to ask for help."

"Oh! You spent the night with her? That is good progress."

"Yes indeed! I spent the night with her *discussing you*. I am going to smoke an entire pack of cigarettes in despair after she goes away. Anyway, you have a surprise visitor today!" said Arjun and the call got disconnected.

"Hello ... hello, I hate call drops," sulked Shiv.

He looked at Tony who was staring at him. He excused himself for a few more minutes and called up his dad.

Then, he sat opposite Tony and asked, "Would you like some coffee while we discuss the plan for today?"

Tony declined, pointed at his watch and said, "It is two in the afternoon. I don't think we can work out a plan. Besides, you have a visitor in the lobby."

"A visitor?" Shiv raised his eyebrows in surprise and called up the lobby. The receptionist confirmed that she was sending a visitor to Shiv's room.

Shiv was only wearing his shorts. He quickly slipped on his white sleeveless T-shirt. There was a knock on the door. Tony opened the door and Shiv's jaw dropped on seeing the visitor.

It was Nysa. She looked more beautiful in person than in the photograph. She was almost five feet eight inches tall, heavy chested and except for a small blemish on her forehead, she had a dusky smooth glowing complexion. She had a beautiful black spot on the side of her slender neck. The brown shades rolled onto her head held her black silky curls behind. Her kohl-lined black eyes moved around the room to find Shiv. She was wearing light blue denims and a red checked shirt.

Time stopped for Shiv. He felt that he had been waiting for this moment his whole lifetime. He had never felt like this before, not for any woman. It was a magical moment.

Shiv could feel his heart pounding in his chest and could almost hear his heartbeats. He took deep breaths to control his emotions. He went to the balcony and took a few breaths of fresh air. He turned and Nysa was standing right opposite him. He was wordless.

"Hi! Do I know you?" he blurted.

"I am not sure. Are you Shiv?" asked Nysa.

He began quivering when Nysa called out his name. "Yes," he managed to mumble.

"You are shaking. I think you should lie down," she said and took him in.

"I am fine. You wanted to see me?"

"Actually, Arjun said you wanted to see me. Also, he has told me about your condition. I am sorry."

"My condition?" asked Shiv surprised. 'What has Arjun told her?' he wondered.

He excused himself and scrolled the messages in his cellphone. He opened the messages from Arjun.

One of the messages read:

Surprise visitor for you! Have told her that you are a terminal cancer patient.

"What!" blurted out Shiv while reading the message.

Nysa rushed and supported him. "Are you alright?"

She helped him lie down and went to fetch some water. Her touch had an electrifying effect on him. He picked up a pillow and kept it on his lap to hide his erection.

Nothing made sense to Tony.

He walked up to Shiv and asked, "What is the matter?"

"Nothing Tony. Just a little complication in my life. I'll sort it out. Both of us will see you tomorrow morning."

"Both? Is she staying?" asked Tony staring at Shiv's pillow.

"I'll make her stay," said Shiv confidently.

Tony eyed the pillow and said, "Well, you do know that you will have to move the pillow some time. I suggest you think of a more permanent solution like a scrotal guard."

Shiv looked embarrassed and diverted Tony by asking, "Why are you wearing gumboots?"

Tony shrugged and said, "You don't have much choice if you have a black cobra stalking you."

Shiv was both shocked and confused.

"Aamir!" He exclaimed.

Tony had a confused look on his face. "Who's that?"

Shiv replied, "Nobody. We will see you tomorrow."

Tony went out, leaving the two alone. Nysa came back with a glass of water.

"Arjun said the hotel didn't have an extra room. I confirmed it. So, I guess I will have to stay here for today. Will that be okay?" asked Nysa.

'Okay? That will be awesome,' thought Shiv.

"Hmm … I'll manage," he told her.

"By the way, Arjun is an awesome guy," said Nysa.

"You like him?" asked Shiv trying to hide his jealousy while feeling the pain that Arjun always felt.

"Yes, he is an attractive and good man."

Shiv threw a lopsided smile and shook his head. She went into the washroom to freshen up.

Shiv called up Arjun, "What do you think you are doing?"

"What are you talking about?" asked Arjun.

"You told Nysa I am going to die?"

"I thought you called to thank me. Anyway, you are welcome."

"You hold that pack of cigarettes for me. I am going to smoke myself up because Nysa finds you attractive."

"Finally, you got a taste of your own medicine," chuckled Arjun.

The call dropped again.

Nysa came back. She had changed into a pink chiffon saree with a halter neck blouse. She is all set to seduce me completely, thought Shiv, pressing the pillow hard again.

He excused himself to freshen up. He was relaxed and in control of himself when he came out wearing a bathrobe. He dressed up while Nysa waited in the balcony. He noticed that Nysa was checking him out. He wore a shaded grey tight fit full sleeve t-shirt with black denims. Nysa walked in and was impressed to see his physique, given his medical condition.

"Hungry?" asked Shiv.

She looked at him seductively and nodded. She walked towards him and sensuously touched his torso.

Shiv held his breath. "For food, I mean," he quickly added.

"Oh!" she replied. "Yes, of course. You are ill and I do understand that you are low on libido because of medicines. Let's eat."

Low on libido? My foot! Shiv silently cursed.

They went to the hotel restaurant and ordered food and mocktails.

"Tell me about you," said Shiv.

"Me? I graduated last year as a clinical psychologist and am appearing for an exam to immigrate to the US."

"Oh! I heard something else."

"That I am a mistress to Mr Mittal? That I am. He is going to fund my education abroad. I have to return his favour. He runs a charitable trust that finances deserving students' education in return for their services. The terms and conditions of the services are clarified only after the students sign the contract. I work as an escort accompanying him to parties and occasions where he is embarrassed to take his illiterate wife."

"Is that all you do? Escorting, I mean. Is it the first time you are doing it? Do you want out?" asked Shiv unable to hide his concern and curiosity.

She raised an eyebrow and replied, "What I do for him is none of anyone's business. Yes, it is my first time. And no, I don't want out because I see the bigger picture of moving out of this place. I have grown up as an orphan and I know the value of being rich and powerful."

"What if I finance your education?"

"In return for what?"

'You' he wanted to reply, but said, "Nothing, just a good deed."

"For the salvation of your dying soul?" she chuckled. "I don't think I am your gateway to heaven. Besides, I believe in keeping my commitments."

"I see," replied Shiv with disappointment in his tone. "What if I wasn't dying?"

"Still the answer would be no."

Shiv looked dejected. I promised to pursue her. I have to keep trying, he convinced himself.

"Does Mittal know you are here?" asked Shiv.

She shook her head, "He is out of country for a few days. Arjun told me about your condition and about how you felt about me. I couldn't break his heart. He was in tears and on his knees. So, I agreed to do a good deed."

Shiv wanted to punch Arjun in his face. What drama!

"What a divine guy! To Arjun," said Shiv raising his glass of mocktail.

"To Arjun," cheered Nysa.

They finished lunch and spent some time in the hotel park. Nysa trotted around the park like a little girl. Shiv got a clear view of the scar on her back. He tried to look at her ankles, but was unable to see them. What am I doing? It was just a dream, he thought.

They settled on a bench eventually.

"Would you accompany me tomorrow to the Khajuraho temples?" asked Shiv.

"Anything you say," replied Nysa. "What is it about me that you wanted so desperately? I did a background check and I know you have had a lot of women."

"I don't know. I just couldn't get you off my mind."

"It didn't seem that way earlier in the room," she said chuckling.

"Oh that? I … I…" hesitated Shiv.

"I what?" asked Nysa smiling.

Shiv looked at her surprised and replied, "I like to go slow."

"Oh," said Nysa. "How slow?" she asked after a while. "You do know that we have limited time. I have to return and your health …"

"Yes, I am aware," said Shiv, his lips stretching into a thin line.

At dinner time, both were not hungry. They had a glass of wine and went back to the room to relax. She changed into a short top with spaghetti straps and comfortable capris. I am going to die of suppressing my urge today, thought Shiv. He had to use a pillow again.

He was sitting on the bed and was mindlessly surfing television channels when she came and sat next to him. She put her head on his shoulders. He went numb. The warmth of the wine in his system wanted him to act by grabbing and crushing her under him, but he resisted. As a reflex action, he stopped changing the television channels. The current channel was showing *The Notebook*. She took away the remote from his hand and said, "My favourite movie."

He sat without making any movement. He got a glimpse of her right ankle and could see a horizontal scar similar to his. Too much of a coincidence, he thought.

In the commercial break, she turned towards him and tried to kiss him. He could not control and kissed her back animatedly for a very long time. He touched her face and neck. He could feel her hands moving on his chest and in his hair.

With great difficulty, he pulled himself back.

"What?" she asked.

"You alright? You are breathless and I can hear your heart thumping loudly. Is it your first time?"

"Of course not."

"We should wait."

"Right, you want to go slow." She got up irritated and went to the bathroom to splash a lot of cold water on her face.

He sat in shock pressing the pillow hard into his groin. I don't have to do this, he tried to convince himself. I can have her. But, if I have her now, I will lose her forever. I have to make her realize that she is exclusively mine. I have to resist, he thought. He pretended to be asleep when she came out. She looked at him and pulled a bed sheet over him.

"Poor guy! Must be the illness," she sighed.

She switched off the television and slept on the sofa. Shiv could not sleep all night. He watched her until the first ray of sunlight lit her face and hair. 'What a sight!' he thought lost in nostalgia.

He changed into his gym wear and headed to the hotel gym to vent out his frustration. She was still sleeping when he returned. She was chewing her cheek from within. She has progressed from biting her lower lip to biting her inner cheek, he thought smiling. He released her cheek and gently stroked it with the back of his hand. He sat beside her for a long time admiring her beauty.

As soon as she moved, he got up and began doing push-ups.

She looked at him and smiled, "Good morning."

He smiled and acknowledged her, while holding his body in a plank position. She looked at him and tried to imagine herself below him. Just then, he began to move his pelvis up and down. She couldn't control and rushed to the bathroom to splash water on her face. He was sitting on the floor sipping water when she returned.

"What's with splashing water on your face? I saw you do that yesterday too," asked Shiv.

"It's nothing. Just to slow me down to your pace. You are hot, I mean, it's very hot," she replied.

"Yes, it is."

"You seem to be very fit, despite the illness. Aren't you supposed to have lost weight and muscle like other cancer patients?"

"I am plain lucky, I think."

Shiv and Nysa met Tony in their hotel lobby. Nysa was wearing a mid-thigh length floral print pink T-shirt with white capris and a white cap. Her hair was tied in a high pony tail and she wore brown shades. Shiv was wearing a half sleeve dark grey t-shirt and white denims. He wore grey shades. Tony was his usual self; he was wearing a red t-shirt, dark blue denims, a Khajuraho stole and black gumboots.

He was delighted to see Shiv and Nysa together. He gave a thumbs-up sign to Shiv.

"You managed to convince her to stay back?" he whispered.

"Yes, I did," replied Shiv.

"Are you wearing the guard?" asked Tony.

Shiv walked away without answering. They headed to the temples. Shiv felt a strange sense of déjà vu on reaching the Kandariya Mahadev Temple. He inspected the sculptures closely, touching and feeling them. He had seen the sculptures before in his dream.

He turned around to look for Nysa. She was standing on the platform next to the main entrance of the temple. She was resting her back against the wall of the temple, a scene he had witnessed before. He walked up to her and stood close, facing her. He put her scattered hair strands behind her ears and kissed her forehead.

"Are you trying to play my big brother? I don't quite get a brotherly feeling when I look at you," she said.

He put both his arms against the temple wall pinning her in between. "What kind of feeling do you get?" he asked moving closer.

"I want to splash water on my face."

"You don't have that option unless you answer my question."

"I ... I."

"I what?" he demanded.

"I ... I am obviously as attracted to you as you are to me. But you are playing difficult to get."

"Because I don't want you to get this," he replied placing her hand on his face. "I want you to get this," he said moving her hand to his heart.

"You are making me uncomfortable," she said with tears in her eyes.

He let her go. A long silence prevailed until they reached the Jain temple. Both of them stood watching the sculpture that Shiv had replicated.

Tony intervened, "Sir, this is the sculpture similar to what you have made. But, look at the right leg of the lady. It is slightly behind as though pulled by something. After you showed me the picture, I enquired about this sculpture. There was no story about it except the fact that the artist who made this sculpture made no other sculpture in this temple."

"I know," replied Shiv, lost in thoughts.

"Are you feeling better now?" Shiv asked Nysa.

"Yes," she replied. "I have grown up in an orphanage and never bonded with anyone. You want to use me, you are welcome, but don't play with my sentiments."

"I am sorry about your childhood, but you have to trust me."

"Why? You are going to die anyway. Then why build up my hopes?"

"Okay. This is going to be difficult for you to digest, but Arjun had lied to convince you to meet me. I am not going to die. Understand?" he said lifting up her chin.

She looked at him surprised, "I am not sure whether to be happy or feel cheated. However, I surely admire Arjun's love for you."

"You ponder over this tonight. We will talk tomorrow. Would you accompany me to Panna National Park tomorrow?"

She nodded unenthusiastically. Shiv directed Tony to make the necessary reservations. They went back to the room. Nysa changed into a silver satin negligee and wore a transparent silver nightshirt over it. Shiv was already in bed and couldn't take his eyes off her when she came out. He pressed the pillow over his groin.

She noticed the pillow and said, "Why don't you too try splashing cold water on your face. It helps."

"Don't need to." He tried to act cool.

"Of course! You are a man in total control of yourself. I can see that," she replied walking out to the balcony.

Shiv was gazing at her voluptuous silhouette outlined in the moonlight. When she turned around to come in, Shiv was standing with a bed sheet in his hand.

He gently draped it around her and said, "Your seductions are exclusively for me."

"Are you sure?" she asked.

He nodded. She walked into the room and dropped the bed sheet and, to Shiv's surprise, the transparent nightshirt too. She stood wearing the silver satin negligee hugging her perfect curves and her smooth creamy body.

Shiv closed his eyes to control himself. After a while, he opened his blazing eyes. Nysa was pouting at him seductively. He picked up the bed sheet and draped it over her again. He hugged her tightly and kissed her face and neck.

He gently carried her, laid her on the bed and closed her eyes. "I want your heart and trust first. Tell me when you're ready to hand over those."

He went to the washroom to splash water on his face. When he came out, Nysa was asleep. He could see that a tear or two had rolled off her eyes. She was chewing her inner cheek on one side. He sat beside her, wiped her tears, released her cheek and kissed her forehead.

"You have no idea what it is to keep my hands off you. I want to cherish you not once, but forever. I have promised you that I'd take care of you forever," he said holding her hand.

Next morning, Nysa was withdrawn.

"Everything alright?" asked Shiv.

"I have decided to not throw myself at you. It is derogatory."

"Good decision. It'll save a lot of water," joked Shiv.

"And spare the pillow from choking," added Nysa. "Besides, Mittal is coming back in two days. I'll have to leave for Mumbai tomorrow."

Shiv raised his eyes from his coffee cup and looked worried. Today is my last chance to convince her, he thought.

Tony had booked a luxury sedan for Shiv. He informed Shiv that though the distance was short, the journey would take two to three hours because of the poor condition of the roads. Shiv and Nysa thanked Tony and bade him goodbye. Shiv offered to pay Tony, but he declined. The driver of the sedan held open the door for them. Once settled and on their way, Nysa was looking out of the window and Shiv was admiring her.

"This is beautiful," she said looking at the picturesque sight.

"Indeed, it is," he replied not taking his eyes off her.

"Can you stop staring?" she said looking out of the window.

"No," he replied and moved closer to her.

"Do you do this to all your women?"

"Do what?"

"Want to own their heart and trust and want them to be exclusively yours."

"No, just to you."

"Why can't we go with the flow and enjoy the moment? Why does it have to be so complicated?"

He rested his head on the back seat and let out a sigh, "You wouldn't understand even if I explained."

"Try me."

He looked at her and continued staring. She shook her head, giving up and looked out of the window. After about an hour's drive, Shiv asked the driver to stop at the nearest restaurant for breakfast. The driver pulled up at a decent looking café off the main road. Shiv gave some money to the driver for breakfast and led Nysa to the café.

The café was surprisingly crowded. It seemed popular. They placed an order and Shiv excused himself to make calls to his father and Arjun. He tried calling his dad, but the phone was switched off. Surprisingly, Arjun's phone was also switched off. He left messages for both of them to call back. He thought of calling Saloni, but decided against it. Instead, he dialled on the landline of his home. No one picked up the call. This was strange. He began to get worried.

"What's the matter?" asked Nysa.

"Nothing, I can't get in touch with my dad. Am worried about him."

"Oh."

He called Saloni. "Hey sweetheart, how are you doing? I... I," he didn't get a chance to speak.

Saloni was bombarding him with questions. She had been worried about him.

"I'll explain when I'm back. I can't get in touch with dad or Arjun. Could you ask them to call back? You too take care ... er ... yes, I miss you too, Saloni."

Nysa was frowning by the time he finished his conversation, "Looks like the exclusivity clause applies only to me. Who was she?"

"A close friend," he replied smiling.

"I see," she seemed dissatisfied with the answer. "I am not hungry anymore," she said getting up.

"Don't be a child. You have eaten nothing after lunchtime yesterday," he said holding her hand.

"I'll wait until you finish … a close friend huh?" she mocked while muttering something and sitting back.

Shiv was amused by Nysa's behaviour. She didn't even realize that she was jealous, he thought. He protectively put an arm around her shoulder when they walked out of the restaurant towards the car park. She liked the way he possessively held her. His gestures shouted out, 'She's mine'.

In the car park, they heard a gunshot. A bullet had just missed them. They panicked and looked in the direction of the sound. Nysa saw somebody moving with a gun pointed in Shiv's direction. Before Shiv realized what was happening, Nysa shouted, "Shiv," and threw herself before him.

A bullet hit her. Shiv screamed, "Mohini!"

She looked at him with doleful eyes and collapsed. He wanted to run in the direction of the killer, but he couldn't leave Nysa bleeding. Nysa lay in a pool of blood. The bullet had injured her right shoulder. She was unconscious. Shiv knew who had fired the gun. The gumboots and the stole had given away the identity of the killer in spite of the mask.

Shiv carried Nysa and rushed to the car. The nearest hospital was at Khajuraho. Throughout the way, he kept pressing her wound to avoid bleeding. He was in tears seeing her in pain. He couldn't lose her, not again.

At the hospital, the surgeon-in-charge apprised Shiv that although the bullet had just grazed Nysa's shoulder, she was still critical due to severe blood loss. She was put under observation for twenty-four hours. Shiv was devastated. The scene of Rudra and Mohini's death kept running in his mind. No! The universe can't be so cruel, he thought.

Next day, the surgeon informed Shiv that Nysa was out of danger, but unconscious, and he could visit her for a while. He was relieved. Her face was pale and lips dry. She was muttering something. Shiv looked at the nurse for an explanation.

The nurse informed, "She has been muttering 'Shiv' all night. She is very religious, I guess."

He nodded and smiled. The nurse excused herself while. Shiv held Nysa's hand and kissed it. He caressed her forehead. Nysa moved a little and opened her eyes.

She looked at Shiv and asked, "Are you okay?"

He nodded mildly and asked, "And you?"

She smiled and then winced in pain.

"Why did you do it?" he whispered.

She looked at him and said, "You wanted my trust. I gave you my life and my soul too."

He was in tears, but managed to ask, "Why?"

"Because I ... I."

"I what?" he whispered.

She rolled her eyes, "Because I am stupid."

He chuckled lightly.

"Was there a hurricane outside?" she asked to lighten his mood.

He looked at her confused.

"What's with your sexy stubble and ruffled hair? Don't do this to me now. I can't even get up and splash water on my face. Will you sprinkle some on my face?" she joked.

"No more splashing water. We will just wait until you recover and then…"

"Then what?"

"Then, I am going to gobble you up," he replied cupping her face in his hands.

"I am waiting to be devoured. You promise you'll never hurt or leave me?"

"Never," he said kissing her hand.

She looked at him longingly and went back to sleep. He vowed to get Tony for this. He got up and decided to look for Tony before she was awake. He went back to the hotel in Khajuraho and made enquiries regarding Tony at the reception. They informed him that Tony lived at the miner's village near Panna National Park.

"Oh! So that would be three hours up and back, right?" he asked.

"No sir, it is less than an hour's drive," informed the receptionist.

"But aren't the roads bad?"

"No sir, the road to Panna National Park is a well-maintained highway."

The driver and Tony were together in this, thought Shiv. The diversion from the highway was a setup. The driver had fled soon after dropping Nysa and Shiv to the hospital. If the driver had a chance, he would have run off earlier, but Shiv had been swift in getting Nysa into the car. Later, he fled with all their belongings.

Shiv tried calling up his dad and Arjun. The phones were still switched off. This time, Saloni's phone was also switched off. He found the timing of the attack and the unavailability of his dad and Arjun very strange. It couldn't possibly be coincidental, he thought.

He hired a car to the miner's village. He was at the village in about forty-five minutes. He enquired about Tony. Somebody directed him to a local tea stall. At the tea stall, he saw Tony sitting and chatting with a few friends. On seeing Shiv, Tony ran in the direction of the forest. Shiv ran after him. When Shiv was about to grab Tony, he pointed a pistol at Shiv. Shiv stepped back seeing the pistol.

"Why did you try to kill Nysa?" he asked.

"Nysa? No, the shot was for you. The dumb girl saved you," replied Tony. "But I can't decide who among the two of you is dumber. You played right into my hands." Tony was laughing.

Shiv saw a black cobra hanging from the tree above Tony's head.

He warned Tony. "There is a black cobra right above you."

"Really? You think I too am dumb?"

Before Tony could say anything else, the cobra fell on Tony and bit his hand that held the pistol. Tony dropped the pistol in shock and pain. The cobra slid away. Shiv had a sense of déjà vu. He looked around. He was in the same forest. He had seen that look of pain on Aamir's face before. Without thinking, he carried Tony on his shoulder and ran towards the village. The villagers revived Tony by giving him an antidote. After a few hours, Tony was better.

He was ashamed of himself on seeing Shiv. "I tried to kill you and you saved me?" he asked with tears rolling down his eyes.

"I acted without thinking," replied Shiv, making no effort to hide his anger.

"I am sorry," said Tony.

"Why did you want to kill me?"

"On instructions from your friend."

"Arjun? That's impossible! You liar!" shouted Shiv in shock.

"I don't know the name of your friend. He calls me from a private number and leaves envelopes of cash at random places."

Why would Arjun do that? For Saloni? No, there is some misunderstanding. It has to be someone else.

"I received you at the airport on his instructions and have been sending him daily updates on you," said Tony.

Shiv suddenly remembered that there were two people carrying placards of his name at the airport, and he had thought that it was a backup.

"I am sorry. I promise to help. You are a good man," said Tony repenting.

"You come to the hospital as soon as you are fit. Right now, I need to get back there," said Shiv and left the place. He reached the hospital in an hour.

*O*n reaching the hospital, Shiv noticed many police officers searching the area. Shiv rushed to the ICCU. The surgeon was nervously talking to one of the police officers.

"Here he comes," said the surgeon pointing at Shiv.

Shiv ran towards them and asked, "Is she alright?"

"Where were you?" asked the surgeon.

Shiv looked at him confused. "What's the matter?"

"Mr Shiv, a while ago, two masked men barged in and kidnapped Nysa at gun point," informed the police officer.

Shiv nearly collapsed on hearing this. "No!" he shouted.

The police officer helped Shiv sit down and offered him some water. I should have stayed here, he thought. Who would want to kidnap Nysa? Arjun tried to get me killed. Could he be involved? No, that's impossible. What would he gain? Was Mittal back and angry on learning that Nysa was two-timing him? Did he kidnap her? Will she be alright? What am I going to do? The thoughts were killing him. He wiped the beads of perspiration collected on his forehead.

His phone battery was dead. He tried to make calls to Arjun, Saloni, and his dad from the hospital landline. He got voice messages that the phones were switched off. He called up his home landline.

This time Mr Bijlani, the housekeeper, picked up the phone. "Sir, where have you been? I have been trying to reach you. Your phone either was out of network or was switched off. You please rush back. Your dad has been hospitalized."

Shiv was in shock again. The day had been full of bad news. This was terrible. Nysa was injured and kidnapped and his dad was in a hospital. He was torn between his duty and love towards both.

He called up Tony and asked if he knew anything about Nysa's kidnapping. Tony denied any knowledge, but pledged to help him. He assured Shiv that he would look into the matter immediately.

Shiv left for Mumbai with a heavy heart. Khajuraho had robbed him of his love for the second time. In addition, he didn't even know if he could trust Arjun anymore. Life is cruel, he thought. It can strip you of everything in a minute. He fell asleep during his flight for a few hours for the first time in the last two days. He rushed to the hospital from the airport.

He met Mr and Mrs Ballad, Saloni's parents, at the hospital. Mr Ballad embraced Shiv.

"What happened?" asked Shiv.

"Two days ago, I received a call from Arjun that Saurabh had a stroke. He asked me to visit Sanyal House immediately. Bijlani and I rushed Saurabh to this hospital. The doctors think his blood pressure shot up and he suffered a brain haemorrhage. They are not sure how long it will take for him to recover," informed Mr Ballad.

"Arjun is not here?"

"Arjun is missing since just after Saurabh suffered the stroke. In fact, Arjun was the last person to see him that day."

"And Saloni?"

"She is in Goa to attend a friend's wedding. I have not been able to contact her."

"Yes, her phone is switched off."

"She did not give me the details of her whereabouts, which is very unlike her. I have put my people at work. Goa is a small place."

Shiv went in to see his dad. Mr. Sanyal looked like a warrior who had collapsed after valiantly fighting a war. Shiv hugged his dad and cried like a baby. The nurse had to pull him away.

Mr Ballad asked, "Would you like to stay at Ballad house? And don't worry about the bills, I'll take care of it."

Shiv was puzzled.

"Arjun has staked legal claim over the house and business. He has the power of attorney," explained Mr Ballad.

Shiv was stunned. So, this was his final goal. It was not only Saloni, but also the business and property, thought Shiv. I have to find Arjun to get back Nysa. He was now sure that Arjun had kidnapped her.

Shiv thanked Mr Ballad for his help and took his leave. He went to Sanyal House to confirm the information given by Mr Ballad. Mr Bijlani asserted Mr Ballad's story. In fact, it was him who had informed Mr Ballad that Arjun was the last person to see Mr Sanyal.

Mr Bijlani politely informed Shiv that as per Arjun's orders, Shiv could no longer stay at Sanyal House. Shiv walked out and wandered aimlessly. He did not know what to do and where to go.

He sat on a bench on the street across Sanyal House and stared blankly at his ex-mansion. He had always viewed the ocean from his house. Today, he had a perspective of his house from the ocean. He felt like drowning himself in the sea. He saw a saint passing by and bystanders paying homages to the holy man. Shiv thought of Devi. Arjun had mentioned that Mr Sanyal often visited Devi and thought that she was a pious woman. Perhaps, she could help.

Shiv used the public transport for the first time in his life. Ms Devi lived in the suburbs. Her bungalow was crowded with visitors lined up to meet her. Shiv had no idea that she was so popular. He stood at the gate wondering if she would recognize him in his current tattered state.

He stood outside her bungalow, contemplating whether he should join the devotees or drop the idea of meeting her. Just then, one of Devi's associates requested Shiv to accompany him. A surprised Shiv followed him. He was led to a guest room. The associate informed him that Devi ji would meet him shortly. He requested Shiv to freshen up and eat. Shiv had a bath and changed into a white kurta and pyjama provided by the associate. Although he was hungry, he was unable to eat due to the immense stress he was under. Thoughts of his dad's health, Nysa's safety and Arjun's deceit tensed him. He looked out of the window. The crowd had dispersed. Perhaps, the visiting hours were over.

From the treatment given to him, Shiv assumed that his dad might have been close to Devi ji. Soon the associate returned and requested Shiv to follow him. This time, Shiv was more observant. He saw that beautiful and valuable artworks decorated the house.

"All these have been gifted to Devi ji?" he asked the associate.

"No! Devi ji never accepts gifts from anyone. She has created these artworks herself," replied the associate.

"Oh!" said Shiv. He was impressed to learn that Devi was not a con fooling people for money.

While climbing down the stairs, Shiv noticed a sculpture of *Shivalinga* with a pair of hands pouring water over it. This sculpture was similar to the one he had seen in his dreams. In his dream, he had made a similar sculpture during his selection test at Khajuraho. This was strange. This was no coincidence, he thought.

Devi was waiting at the dinner table for Shiv. She dismissed all her associates as soon as Shiv was seated.

Shiv greeted her and said, "Thanks for having me."

"My pleasure, son! I wasn't able to gain your confidence in the past and missed an opportunity. I couldn't possibly miss it again."

Shiv looked at her perplexed.

"I know you don't believe in past lives." She smiled. "Did you like the sculpture on the stairway? One of my students had sculpted it in the *past*. I recreated it."

Shiv looked at her and mumbled, "Master Chiru… No! That's impossible."

Devi continue to smile.

She knew Shiv had not eaten in the room. "Son, if any of your problems are going to be solved by staying hungry, I'll join you. If not, eat your food, so that we have enough energy to find solutions to your problems."

Shiv did not argue and ate his meal. He felt a sudden sense of relief and hope. He felt that Devi could help him.

"As you might be aware, all our souls are in different stages of maturity. You are progressing towards Dharma. You are feeling bound by your duties. You are a good man and you will make it through," she said.

"How? Where do I start?"

"Don't worry about Saurabh. He will be fine. You follow your heart."

"Nysa … she has been kidnapped."

"So, go and find her where you lost her. Be witty and alert. Don't underestimate your enemy."

"You know who is the enemy?"

"I do, but I can't break the rules of the universe by revealing the future. Besides, the future is constantly reshaping depending on our present karma."

"Perhaps, a clue might help."

"It's your battle, your destiny, you have to fight it. I am only a soul guide."

After the meal, she told Shiv to relax and be ready the next morning to visit his dad before leaving for Khajuraho. She made the necessary arrangements for his travel and provided him with money. Shiv felt strangely relaxed and slept well. Next morning, he visited his father and took Devi's blessing before parting.

Three days earlier, when Shiv had called up Saloni from the restaurant before Nysa was shot, Saloni decided to visit Sanyal House to check on Mr Sanyal and Arjun. She found it strange that both their phones were switched off.

She reached Sanyal House and noticed that the gate was guarded by unknown armed men, who looked like goons. Saloni was familiar with the security staff of Sanyal House and was sure that she had never seen these men. She decided to play it safe and watched the house from a distance across the street seated in her car. It was a busy street and many cars were parked. Hence, she could remain unnoticed.

After a while, an ambulance arrived at Sanyal House. She assumed that somebody was unwell in Sanyal House. But who? She wanted to rush in to help, but her instincts stopped her.

Moments later, her dad arrived and entered Sanyal House. He emerged along with Mr Bijlani and some men from the ambulance team who were carrying Mr Sanyal on a stretcher. She could hold back no more. She jumped out of her car to help. As she was crossing the street, she noticed that the armed goons were making phone calls. She thought it would be safer to speak to her dad and reach the hospital directly rather than entering Sanyal House in the current situation. She wondered why Arjun wasn't here to help Mr Sanyal.

After the ambulance left, she too decided to leave. Just then, she saw four armed men coming out of Sanyal House. She recognized one of the men. It was Arjun! Why was he wearing a security guard's uniform similar to that of the goons? They got into a car. She saw that the armed men were pointing guns and pushing Arjun into the back seat of their car. Oh god! They were kidnapping Arjun, she thought.

She followed the car at a safe distance. She decided to wait before calling the police or her dad fearing that she would lose sight of the goon's car in the traffic.

Saloni was a huge Hollywood fan. She decided to put all that knowledge into practice. The car entered the parking lot of a commercial complex. Scared that she would get noticed, she didn't follow the car into the building. She researched on the internet to find the offices that operated in the complex. She picked up the name of a call center hoping that it would be open any time of the day.

At 8 p.m., Saloni noticed that many employees were coming out of the building. The security guards of the commercial complex were busy checking the cars of employees leaving and entering the building. She parked her car outside the complex and slipped into the gate unnoticed, when the guards were busy.

In the lobby, because she did not have an identity card, she was asked to enter the name of the office she was visiting. She quickly scribbled the name of the call center. Instead of the elevator, she used the fire exit and went to the parking lot.

As most employees of the earlier shift had left and the new shift was yet to come in, there were only a few cars in the parking lot. Saloni easily located the car she was following. She looked around. There were no cameras and security guards. She looked into the car. It was empty. The goons had moved Arjun from here, she thought. She knocked on the car boot to make sure he was not locked up in there. She whispered his name, but there was no response. She tried calling his cell phone, but there was no signal in the parking lot.

They had taken him somewhere into the building, she thought. How will I find out? She came out of the parking lot to call for help. But before that, she had to be sure that he was in the building.

The office building had fifteen floors. By the time she would finish checking each floor, Arjun could be killed or moved again. She had to think of something fast. She looked for parking stickers indicating the office name on the kidnapper's car. She had no luck. She thought for a while and noted the car and the parking lot's number. She also noted the number of a Mercedes parked in the next parking lot.

Going back to the lobby, she spoke confidently to the security guard, "The car with number MH08 XY 1442 parked in lot number E14 has scratched my boss's car parked in E13. My boss wants to know who it belongs to."

She acted convincingly angry and pressurized the security guard for urgent information. The guard asked her to give her boss's car number to verify. She promptly blurted out the number. He seemed to have no doubt now.

He checked the parking lot allotment and told her that the car owner belonged to Synchron Technologies on the eighth floor. She thanked him and moved away. Before her anxiety would become evident, she ran back into the fire exit to catch her breath and plan further. She hoped and prayed that the information was useful. Resuming her poise, she moved into the lobby and took the elevator.

Saloni checked herself out in the elevator mirror. She was wearing a dark green sleeveless floral print top and light blue jeans. The blue sling hanging across her shoulder added to her casual look. Too casual to appear for an interview, she thought. She would have to give some other excuse to enter the office.

The scene on the eighth floor was chaotic. Each employee was being checked thoroughly and was allowed to enter only after a thumb print confirmation. Was it possible for the goons to bring Arjun here without being noticed? she thought. No, they must have taken him to some other place. What do I do now? She went back to the lobby.

She scanned the names of offices on the name board in the lobby, hoping to find a familiar name. She saw that Synchron Technologies had an office on the ninth floor too. That's the one, she thought. She took the elevator again to the eighth floor, alighted from it and took the fire exit to the ninth floor.

The floor was empty. Out of the three offices on that floor, one belonged to Synchron Technologies. She went closer to the office door to ascertain any indication of movement inside the office. She could see a faint light emitting out from the bottom of the main door. She heard a few footsteps and muffled sounds.

Somebody was definitely inside, she thought. She decided to call the police for help. But what if Arjun wasn't here? The kidnappers would be alerted and could harm Arjun. She couldn't take any chances. She made up her mind to confirm before calling.

As she stood with her ear glued to the main door of the office, the door knob began to move. Somebody was trying to come out! She panicked. She knew that she would not make it to the fire exit in time. There was another door next to the office door. She tried opening it. It was open! She quickly slipped inside and switched off her mobile. The fact that mobile phones gave away the location of actors in movies by ringing at the most inconvenient time irritated her.

She heard somebody coming out of the main door, a male voice saying, "I'll take these papers to the boss. You two keep watching."

She saw a shadow passing across the base of her door. The man took the elevator and then there was silence again. The only sound she could hear was her own heavy breathing. She looked around to see where she was hiding. It was a closet containing cleaning equipment. She looked at the ceiling and instantly knew what she was going to do to confirm if Arjun was here.

She climbed up the cleaning staircase to reach the ceiling of the closet. She had seen in movies that a common air conditioning duct ran through the ceiling and connected all the rooms in offices. She thought she could peep and check if it was feasible to move around in this one.

The four corners of the opening of the duct were screwed such that two opened from inside and two from outside to enable maintenance staff to approach from any side.

This was great! she thought. She opened two screws using a Swiss knife she always carried in her purse. Sliding the lid by rotating it over the other two screws, she created a space big enough for her to crawl in.

Saloni peeped inside the duct. It was a big space. The air conditioners were switched off because the offices were closed at this hour. She crawled slowly without making any noise towards the office with lights.

While passing across the reception of Synchron Technologies, she peeped through the grilled vents and noticed that the two goons who had abducted Arjun were fast asleep on comfortable looking sofas. This was good, she thought.

She moved ahead unaware that the ceiling inside the office was made of thick acrylic and her shadow was vividly visible from the dimly lighted room. But fortunately, both the goons were fast asleep. After a couple of empty cabins, she was right above the cabin where Arjun was held. He was bound to a chair with his hands and legs tied and his mouth duct-taped. Bingo! she thought.

He rolled his eyes when he noticed the vividly distracting shadow of someone crawling across the ceiling in an effort to remain hidden. That's silly, he thought. He never expected the person to be Saloni.

She opened the inner screws of the grilled window on the ceiling of the cabin and slid the lid across the other two screws. Arjun was shocked to see Saloni. She waved out to him and flashed an ear-to-ear smile. He looked at the door worried that the noise would bring the goons in. She took off her five-inch heels and left them in the duct. Taking support of the edges of the duct, she hung herself low, and landed softly without making any noise.

"Hi," she whispered.

Arjun nodded his head to acknowledge.

"Oh!" she said and took out the Swiss knife from her bag to cut his rope and ducts.

"What are you doing here?" he whispered harshly.

"Oh! I expected words of gratitude. I was on my daily evening walk in the duct and saw you, so I came down for a courtesy greeting."

"Okay. I am sorry. Thank you, but you should have called for help instead of putting yourself in danger. What if the goons were awake?"

"Hmm. That is a good idea. You wait here and I'll go back through the duct and fetch help. And, how did you know that the goons were sleeping?"

"Oh, that … er … just a wild guess," he said looking at the acrylic ceiling while rolling his eyes. "Let's get out of here."

"That would be a sensible thing to do."

"Too much Hollywood," he muttered to himself.

"You said something?"

"Nah … nothing."

They looked around for things they could assimilate to help them climb back. The chair was their only available tool. Arjun stood on the chair and tried to reach the ceiling. It was too high for his grip. He asked Saloni to join him on the chair. He held her at her waist and lifted her effortlessly. She reached the ceiling and gripped the edges of the duct. She was surprised by his strength and his muscular but gentle grip.

"Now what?" she asked raising her eyebrows from the duct.

He looked around and then finely balanced himself on the hand rest of the chair. He was still short of reaching the ceiling by a few centimeters.

"I think you should go back and call for help," he said giving up.

"I have an idea," she sparkled.

"From Hollywood?"

"No, this one is original."

The next minute, Arjun was wearing her five-inch heels and balancing himself on the hand rest. This time he reached the edges easily and pulled himself up.

"That was great!" he complimented her. "But, how do you walk on these all day long?"

"A woman's life ain't easy, mister," she said smiling.

"You bet," said Arjun handing back her stilettos.

They crawled through the ceiling. He could see her hips sway left and right as she moved. Oh man! She has an attitude even while crawling through a duct, he smiled. She climbed down the staircase and he followed her.

The closet was too small for two people. For the first time, he was standing so close to her. She was beautiful, he thought. He looked into her eyes and said, "Thank you." For the first time, she felt something for him. For the first time, she felt something stir within her by the way he looked at her. For the first time, he saw her blushing because of him.

He partially opened the closet door to check if the corridor was secure. They stepped out and tiptoed to the fire exit. They ran down until the fifth floor. She gestured him to halt.

"It's two a.m. Stepping out at this hour will raise suspicion. The cafeteria is on the fourth floor. I'll go and check if it is safe for us. Besides, I am not sure if you can enter dressed like a security guy."

"Oh, this." He had completely forgotten about his attire.

He quickly removed the shirt. He was wearing a half sleeve dark blue t-shirt beneath. She cleaned all the dust on her, wiped her face, did her hair, and went to the fourth floor.

The cafeteria was crowded. Break time, she thought. She noticed that the employees were using their identity cards to unlock the cafeteria door. She befriended an unassuming guy and borrowed his id card. He was more than delighted to help a pretty damsel in distress. She went back to the exit and signalled Arjun to come.

In the cafeteria, Saloni and Arjun settled down in an inconspicuous corner. Arjun couldn't believe that a few minutes ago, he was held hostage and now he was sitting and having coffee with the love of his life. *She's not just beautiful, she has guts too,* he thought.

"So, tell me the full story," said Saloni.

Arjun sipped his coffee and began, "I went to Sanyal House in the morning for Mr Sanyal's signatures on some important documents. I was worried because Mr Sanyal's phone was switched off even though he wasn't travelling. So, I decided to check on him."

Saloni noticed that a lot of female employees were looking at Arjun with admiration. Arjun acknowledged each one of them by smiling in between the conversation. She respected the fact that he was a 'gentleman' and a loyal friend. Surprisingly, she was jealous of the other women trying to score with him.

"Mr Sanyal was in his bedroom. At first, I thought he was asleep. But, when I tried to awaken him, I noticed that he was unable to breathe, his face was contorted and he appeared to be in distress. I called for an ambulance immediately and asked your dad to come to Sanyal House for help. Then, I called out for help and Mr Bijlani came rushing in. Mr Bijlani said that Mr Sanyal had come down for breakfast and had gone back to his room to dress up. Hence, he did not check on him. The ambulance and your dad arrived soon. I thought of collecting Mr Sanyal's medical reports before rushing to the hospital. Therefore, I sent your dad and Mr Bijlani ahead with the ambulance to save time."

He sipped his coffee and continued, "As soon as they left, some thugs surrounded me. I believe they were already hiding in the house. They had guns, so I did not put up a fight. They asked me to wear the security uniform shirt and brought me out at gunpoint. You know the rest. How did you find me?"

Saloni was closely watching him while he was talking. How did I not notice him before? she wondered.

She broke eye contact, looked around and began her side of the story, "I received a call from Shiv that he could not get through your and Mr Sanyal's phones. He asked me to visit Sanyal House. I found it strange and immediately took off to check. On reaching, I noticed that the security guards at the gate were unfamiliar and heavily armed. I found that alarming. So, judging the situation from my Hollywood experience, I decided to sit back and observe from my car."

"Hmm ... good call. Watching too many Hollywood movies may not be such a bad thing," Arjun commented.

She smiled. "After the ambulance left, the thug security guards continued to stand at the gate. I then saw some goons emerging from the house. I could have easily mistaken you to be a member of their team from the distance I was watching, but I saw the Rolex watch and the silver bracelet that you always wear. So, on inspecting closely, I realized that you were being kidnapped. I followed you here."

"You identified me from my bracelet and watch? You know what I wear. I mean... you have noticed!"

She too was surprised that she had observed such details about him. "Yeah... I mean... er... I know you for so many years, so..." she managed to reply.

"But the watch and bracelet are only a month old." He changed the topic to avoid embarrassment to her. "Is your car in the parking lot?"

"No, it's outside the complex."

"Okay, so what do we do next? Any thoughts?"

"Why don't we use this id card and stay hidden in the eighth-floor office until this shift leaves. We can leave with the crowd and go unnoticed. I bet they won't look for us in their own office. This place is the first they will search."

"The eighth-floor office belongs to them?"

"Both eighth and ninth floor offices are labelled under the same company 'Synchron Technologies', so I guess it belongs to them."

"I have heard that name in some context, but am unable to recollect," he said trying to think hard.

"You are too stressed right now," she said pressing his hand.

"How did you manage the id card?"

"Used my charm," replied Saloni proudly tilting her head slightly behind.

Arjun wasn't amused by her answer. They emerged from the cafeteria along with the crowd and went to the eighth-floor office. At the reception of that office, Arjun used his charming smile and good looks to get them in.

They found their way to an open working area. It was an open terrace with a few working tables and chairs. Some sofas and swings were also arranged for employees to relax during their breaks. The terrace was deserted, probably because the employees were just back from a break or because of the unearthly hour. Arjun surveyed the place and found a corner that was not under CCTV surveillance.

"Good thinking," appreciated Saloni.

They sat for a while and fell asleep. Arjun was awakened by the bright morning sun. He looked at his watch. It was nine a.m. He looked at Saloni. She was sleeping peacefully resting her head on his shoulder. He did not have the heart to wake her up. He gently stroked her arm to awaken her. She got up with a startle.

"It's okay," he said trying to calm her down. "We need to get moving before somebody spots us."

He handed over the id card to the receptionist saying, "I found this lying around. Could you return it to the owner please?"

It was easier to get out of the building than it was to get in. Soon, both were seated in Saloni's car.

"Where should I drop you?" asked Saloni.

"Nowhere. The thugs will look for me at all the expected places, including my home and the hospital. They have already ransacked my house and stolen the power of attorney documents."

"Power of attorney documents?"

"Yeah. They made me sign some documents staking legal claim on Mr Sanyal's property and business because he is not in a condition to make decisions. I believe Shiv's life is also in danger. So, it's best that I remain hidden until I contact Shiv. They can't proceed with the legal stake if they don't have me in person."

"Oh, I see. How about staying low at my place?"

"Not a good idea. You too stay away from your house for a while. Sooner or later in the day, they will figure out from the surveillance cameras that you were involved in my escape. You can also be targeted. Drive straight to the hospital and ask your dad for help, or stay with me, but stay safe… please."

"The thugs have taken away your wallet and phone. How are you going to manage? Why don't you use my card and phone?"

"It's best that I don't get tracked through these devices. And money? I'll manage. Don't' worry. I'll be fine."

"I was thinking I should accompany you. I could be helpful," Saloni said.

His face brightened by her offer, but only for one moment until she added, "I am worried about Shiv."

"Oh! Of course! It's about Shiv. I promise I'll get him back safely for you. Thank you for saving my life for Shiv," he said bitterly and hurried out of the car.

She regretted instantaneously for bringing up Shiv in the conversation, but she didn't know what other reason to give for sticking around with him. She always knew that Arjun had a thing for her, but didn't expect him to be so sensitive. She felt a sense of pain by the way he left her. She continued observing him from the side mirror of her car. He hailed a cab. She reflexively turned around her car and followed him.

The cab stopped at a suburban five-star hotel. He went inside and came out with a woman to pay for the cab. Saloni was curious to know what he was doing there without any money. Perhaps, he was with a friend, she thought. She decided to find out.

She switched on her phone and messaged her dad that she was leaving for Goa for a friend's wedding and would contact him later. She switched it off again, parked her car at an inconspicuous place and walked into the hotel.

The gatekeeper of the hotel greeted Saloni.

"I am with the guy who just came in a while ago," she said.

"Oh, the singer?" he asked.

"Er... yeah," she replied, trying to hide her surprise.

"You are going to sing romantic duets with him at the party?"

"Er... not exactly. I am here to help him with other things."

"No problem madam. You can meet Mr Anuj, the party organizer. You enquire about him at the reception."

"Thanks."

Arjun, singing and romance! This is getting interesting, she thought.

She went to the reception and said, "I am here for the party."

"Ma'am, there are five parties today. Could you help me with more details?" requested the receptionist.

"The one that is organized by Mr Anuj."

"All of them are."

"Well, I am with the singer who just came in," informed Saloni and hoped that the receptionist wouldn't ask for more details.

"Oh, you mean Arjun?" said the receptionist grinning. "He is such a charmer."

"Indeed! He is," replied Saloni raising her eyebrows and wondering how Arjun managed to charm most women he met.

"The party starts at 1 p.m. on the third floor. Do you want me to direct you to Arjun? He is rehearsing for his performance with his team at the same venue."

"No, thank you. I'll find my way."

While wandering about in the hotel, she caught a glimpse of herself in a mirror displayed on a decorative pillar in the lobby. She looked completely beaten down. I can't look like this ever, she thought.

She went to the hotel boutique and brought herself a decent party gown using her credit card. She knew that Arjun had warned her against using her credit card, but there was no way she was going to let him see her like this.

She went to the rest room and freshened up. She was glad that she always carried some basic make-up with her. She checked herself out in a mirror and was satisfied. Why do I want to look good for Arjun, she wondered? It's just that I always want to look good. Nothing to do with Arjun, she convinced herself.

She went to the hotel restaurant and had some breakfast and coffee. A little after 1 p.m., she entered the party hall along with some other guests.

From the decoration in the hall, it was evident that it was a birthday party for someone named 'Priya'. Why was Arjun going to sing romantic songs for Priya? She missed a beat and felt a little gloomy. She sat in a corner with a glass of wine to avoid being noticed. Soon the room was buzzing with excited guests.

She overheard one of the guests whispering, "He is going to surprise her by proposing."

She felt a pang of jealousy and didn't want to stay there anymore to watch Arjun go down on his knees for some other woman. She hated herself for not feeling happy for Arjun. All along, she had known about his feelings for her, but never reciprocated. And now, when he seemed to have moved on, she didn't want him to. She wanted to know him better.

Fate has strange ways, she thought. She slowly gulped her wine and moved out of the venue. Just a while after she stepped out, she heard Arjun singing.

He began with her favourite song, 'Part-time lovers' by Stevie Wonder. His voice was deep, honest and sexy. She couldn't resist and turned back to the hall. The hall was crowded by now. She could hardly get a glimpse of Arjun. She chose to sit in a corner from where she could see him clearly.

He was wearing a bright yellow shirt with its sleeves rolled up slightly, a black waistcoat and a pair of black trousers. He was clean-shaven and looked like a college student. His body language showed no evidence of the stressful night he had just spent.

Love can do wonders, she thought. The few dance moves that he made while singing were sexy and had all the young girls from the crowd ogling and hooting.

He moved to the next song 'I just called to say I love you' by Stevie Wonder again. She looked around to get a glimpse of Priya. She didn't have to make any guesses because Arjun was standing right beside Priya and coaxing her to dance. Priya looked ravishing. She was wearing a red gown. She was tall, had waist length curly hair and glowing skin. They looked good together.

Saloni couldn't understand why she had a feeling of impending doom. She felt that some part of her happy world was coming to a shattering end. She had experienced heartaches before, but this was different and severe.

Saloni moved to the bar area and sat with her back towards the crowd. She had noticed how the girls were gawking at Arjun. A few songs were sung by other guests too. Then, Arjun sang Bryan Adam's 'Everything I do I do it for you'.

What a range! she thought. She was surely deranged and blind to not have noticed him all along. By now, Saloni had drowned her sorrows in ample amount of alcohol.

His next number, 'Just the way you are' by Bruno Mars had her weeping bitterly. She turned to see him. He was dancing and moving around Priya. She turned back.

Suddenly, she heard a loud cheer from the crowd.

Oh god! Is he on his knees? I can't watch this. She decided to move out, but instead, she magnetically moved towards him. The honesty of his voice was touching. She noticed that he was holding a man by his arm and bringing him to the dais. She was feeling dizzy by now. What's happening? The crowd cheered "Rohan... Rohan."

Arjun handed over the mike to Rohan to sing a couple of lines and then continued singing. Saloni was confused. Had she missed something at the beginning of the show?

By now, Arjun had noticed Saloni. He moved closer to her and sang fixing his eyes on her. She felt that he was singing for her. She stood watching him as if there was no one else in the room. The song ended and Arjun began singing 'Marry you' by Bruno Mars.

The crowd cheered louder. A few couples got up and joined Arjun in a rehearsed dance sequence. The show was beautiful. By the end of the song, Rohan was on his knees with a ring in his hand for Priya. Saloni was relieved. She was flashing a broad smile and applauding.

As soon as Priya said 'Yes', young girls from the party were all over Arjun. At least fifteen girls had mobbed him. Saloni tried to pull away the girls, but they did not budge. They had to be forcibly pulled away by the hotel staff. Arjun's face and neck were covered with lipstick marks. Saloni was burning with jealousy.

Arjun disappeared from the room, cleaned himself, and came back. Saloni was waiting at the bar.

"Hi," he said. "You were on your morning walk and dropped in to say hello?"

"No," she chuckled. "Actually, I was stalking you."

"Really?"

"You don't want to know why?"

"No, I'd like to remain deluded that you came in for me. I am in a good mood."

"Because of all those girls?"

"No, because of you," he said looking at her in the eye.

She lost her smile and became serious.

"Gotcha," he said quickly snapping his fingers at her and began laughing.

"Oh," she laughed and tried to prevent tears from flowing out of her eyes.

"You are a surprise package. Didn't look like your first performance," she said.

"It wasn't. I occasionally perform with the band at Blueberry Club. Today, it was for a buddy."

"I loved your moves."

"They were well-practiced."

"You are being modest."

Just then, one of the hotel staffers informed Arjun that his requested table for two was ready.

"Would you please join me?" he asked.

"I'd be honoured," she replied taking his arm.

"I know you are worried about Shiv. I thought of lying low today and starting tomorrow," he said.

"I came back for you," she snapped at him.

He frowned, "I think you've had too much wine."

"That's because when I came in I thought you were going to propose to Priya."

"So?"

"So ... never mind."

Arjun wasn't sure if Saloni meant what he understood.

At the lunch table, Saloni said, "I didn't know you could sing. What else have I missed?"

"A lot... some missed and some ignored facts."

She looked away. Suddenly, he got up, pulled her by her arm and took her to a corner.

"What is it?" she asked.

"The thugs are here," he warned.

"Oh no! I had switched on my mobile and used my credit card."

"We have to move, now," he said and led her outside, hiding behind the crowd.

"Because your phone was switched off, I tried calling your dad. He didn't pick up my call. I guess he is angry because of the false stake thing," said Arjun on their way out of the hotel.

"Why were you trying to call?"

"I was worried about you. I left you abruptly. I am sorry."

"I forgive you," she replied.

Her face looked flushed with all the alcohol she had consumed. Arjun had to support her because she was stumbling. They hailed a cab and left the place.

In the cab, Saloni was unable to contain herself. By now, the alcohol had complete control over her. Arjun had never seen her like this. Not even when she was depressed over Shiv's multiple affairs. She kept humming the romantic numbers that Arjun had sung. She was trying to wipe off imaginary lipstick marks from Arjun's face.

"You have got one here, one here. How dare they kiss you?"

"Why do you care?" he asked her.

"I didn't before … but …" she mumbled before passing out.

Next day, she was awakened by Arjun who was gently calling out her name. She opened her eyes and saw him standing beside her.

She looked around at the unfamiliar place. "Where are we?"

"On the outskirts of Mumbai, in my farmhouse."

"You have a farmhouse?" she asked rubbing her eyes.

"Not many people know about it. I thought we could hide here for a day."

She looked at her clothes. She was wearing a white cotton shirt and pyjamas, probably belonging to Arjun.

"My clothes? You changed them? You…" she swallowed her words.

Before he could reply, there was a knock on the door.

"Please come in Rosy," shouted Arjun.

A pleasant looking woman in her late fifties came in with breakfast and coffee.

"I thought you would need help with her," said Rosy.

"Thank you for your thoughtfulness. She certainly needs help," replied Arjun.

Before going out, he walked towards Saloni and said, "Well, I am not as shady as Mr Christian Grey, Miss Anastasia Steele."

She was shocked by his comment. Is he a Hollywood fan too, she wondered? Rosy served Saloni her breakfast in the room.

"It's noon, but Arjun sir told me not to wake you up early. How are you feeling today?" she enquired.

"These clothes ...?" She looked at Rosy questioningly.

"Oh these? They belong to Arjun sir. We didn't have anything feminine here. You are the first woman friend visiting us. In fact, you are the first friend who has ever visited here."

"Does he come here often?"

"Arjun sir likes to spend solitary time here. He comes here once or twice every month."

Saloni smiled at this mysterious guy she thought she knew well. "He got these for you to wear now. He was up early and went to the nearby market to get these," informed Rosy handing over a bag to Saloni.

Saloni thanked Rosy. She freshened up and settled to have breakfast. She was wearing black jeans and a pink cotton shirt. The size fitted her well. Rosy had washed her undergarments and kept them in the bag.

"Was I unconscious when I came in yesterday?" asked Saloni.

"Not quite. Arjun sir carried you upstairs. You were humming some songs and trying to hug and… er… kiss. You were not quite yourself is what sir said. So, I helped you change your clothes. Arjun sir asked me to stay with you in case you needed any help at night, but you were knocked out," said Rosy and handed Saloni a cup of coffee.

Saloni felt guilty for doubting Arjun's intentions. After breakfast, she wandered around the house to find him. It was a two-storey house. She had spent the night in the guest bedroom on the top floor. He carried me up these stairs? She was impressed.

The more she knew him, the more she liked him. Like a fool, she had waited for Shiv to reciprocate without actually analyzing her feelings for him. She had a sense of loyalty for Shiv. She felt indebted to him. But why? She had no idea. Her feelings for Arjun were different. She longed to spend time with him. She was beginning to trust him and enjoy his company.

She peeped into the rooms on the ground floor. One of the rooms was a gym. Rosy was busy in the kitchen on the ground floor. The other room was latched from outside.

Saloni tried to unlatch the door when Rosy interrupted, "That one is always latched. It is his personal den. No one goes in there."

The living room was huge with wooden décor. The terrace on the ground floor had a two-seater swing. Several pots of flowering plants lined the edge of the big terrace. Some decorative brass vessels kept in a corner gave a rustic look to the terrace.

The terrace had a few stairs leading to the lawn. She saw Arjun sitting on a chair below a huge umbrella in the lawn. Several empty chairs were placed beside him. He was wearing a pair of headphones and was enjoying some music. She had never seen him relax before.

She didn't want to disturb him, not before she inspected the whole place. The lawn was lined by huge trees. She could not see what lay beyond the tall boundary walls behind the trees. She walked outside around the house. She peeped into the window of the room that she could not open. She saw some photographs decorated on one of the walls. Some were family photographs and others were that of Arjun with Shiv and Mr Sanyal. She recognized a photograph of Arjun with Shiv and herself. She felt happy that he considered her a part of his life. One of the walls had a curtain over it. She moved further ahead towards the other rooms. Just after she moved away from the room, a soft breeze moved the curtain exposing huge photographs of Saloni in various poses and expressions.

Saloni was impressed with the simple beauty of the house. She walked towards Arjun and sat on an empty chair beside him.

He removed his headphones and asked, "Took a good look?"

"I didn't realize you were watching," she replied biting her lip.

"I wasn't. You just happened to be in my field of vision."

"Do we have any plans?"

"Yes, we do. I will go to Khajuraho without alerting the thugs and you will go to your dad. I will safely drop you there first and then proceed."

"I am not going anywhere. I plan to stick with you."

"It could be dangerous. Besides, I will take a bus to Khajuraho to avoid alerting the goons. Not sure if you could manage that."

"If you can, why can't I?"

"I am not doubting your capabilities after the kidnapping night, but I don't want to put you in danger."

"You are not going anywhere without me," she said stubbornly and looked away.

She missed noticing a trace of a smile on Arjun's face.

In the evening, Saloni and Arjun boarded a luxury bus destined to Jhansi.

"What if Shiv isn't in Khajuraho? He could have come to Mumbai after learning about his dad's health," she asked.

"He had come and has gone back. I suspect trouble," replied Arjun.

"You called him up?"

"No, just gathered some information from reliable sources. If he has been to the hospital, he must have got the news of my false legal stake. I have to see him in person to explain. He has taken the morning flight to Khajuraho."

"Why did he go back to Khajuraho?"

"For Nysa, I think."

"Nysa?"

Arjun realized that Saloni was not aware that Shiv was with Nysa in Khajuraho. He repented immediately.

"She is just a friend."

She nodded and said, "Arjun, I am not sure why, but I am not as upset as I should be."

Although Arjun was used to travelling by public transport in his younger days, it was a first-hand experience for Saloni.

"How did you manage the money?" asked Saloni.

"I met a few friends at the party yesterday. They were more than happy to help."

"Ah, yesterday reminds me of the girls who mobbed you. Is that a common scene?" asked Saloni trying to hide her jealousy.

"Oh! You mean the kisses? Yes, that is the scene after each of my performances," replied Arjun smiling mischievously.

"I usually wind up with a date for the evening and requests for many more on my phone. My phone has been switched off since yesterday, so I missed the requests."

"You missed the requests? You enjoy those?" asked Saloni widening her eyes.

"Yeah, I surely do. I have got to keep my options open. Someday, I might meet the one for me."

"Don't get me wrong, but I thought that you had a thing for me," she said blushing.

"You knew about it? I do … I mean I did, but I have moved on."

"Oh, okay, that's good," she tried to hide her disappointment.

She wanted to tell him that she was beginning to develop feelings for him and that she had realized that she was never in love with Shiv. However, she held back due to fear of rejection and ridicule.

"Will you let me know?" she asked.

"What?" he questioned.

"When you find the one," she said looking down.

"Of course, I will. We will all celebrate together. You, Shiv, her and me. You can relax now."

He was enjoying teasing her. He knew that she had started liking him. Destiny had brought her to him so that she could know him better. The bus stopped at a tiny restaurant for dinner. Saloni was a little at unease and Arjun knew that she was uncomfortable, but explained that they had no choice.

"For Shiv," he said.

She felt like Arjun had stabbed her heart with a dagger. She was angry and hurt, but held back.

All these years, like Arjun, she too was under the misconception that she was in love with Shiv. It wasn't Arjun's fault to assume that she still loved Shiv. However, she was hurt to hear it from Arjun. She was tempted to clarify her stand about Shiv, but she didn't want Arjun to judge her character. She didn't want him to think that she had fallen for him after just spending a couple of days with him. She felt a sweet pain for Arjun. Strangely, she was enjoying the pain and wanted more.

After Arjun returned from paying the restaurant bill, he noticed that Saloni wasn't in her place. He looked around for her. Just then, a small girl tugged at his trousers and pointed towards the back door. Arjun rushed there with lightning speed. Saloni was being dragged by the three thugs who had held him captive a couple of days ago. They had guns in their hands.

Arjun noted that one of the thugs had pointed a gun at Saloni's forehead. Another thug had put his arm around Saloni's waist and the third one had his hand on her shoulder. Arjun was burning with anger.

"Let her go. You want me, you've got me," he said threatening the goons.

"She was not a part of the plan, but she invited herself to the party. Now, it is our turn to enjoy. We are going to take you along to watch," said one of the goons laughing.

The thug tightened his grip on Saloni's waist and the other thug's hand began moving lower on Saloni's back. Saloni was wincing in discomfort. Like a flash of lightning, Arjun kicked and knocked off the guns on the floor.

"No one dares to touch my girl," he muttered to himself and within seconds, he knocked out the goons with masterstrokes of martial arts.

All the three thugs were lying unconscious on the floor. Saloni ran towards Arjun and hugged him tightly. He restrained himself from hugging her back. He held her by her hand and they hurried outside for the bus. The bus had left with their belongings. Arjun sat down distressed when another bus driver approached him.

"I saw what happened. Would you two like a lift to Orcha?" he offered.

Arjun agreed after verifying that it was safe. He thanked the bus driver. In the bus, Arjun was tensed and lost in deep thoughts. Saloni looked at him with guilt. She had tears in her eyes.

"It's because of me," she said.

He looked at her, "How so?"

"While you were asleep in the earlier bus, I switched on your mobile."

"No," he nodded. "You are not so dumb."

"Sometimes the heart wins over the brain."

"Oh! Great!" he exclaimed sarcastically. "You never believed that I actually intend to help out Shiv. So, you tried calling him up. You thought that I love you so much that I would never lead you to him. Well! You are wrong. I would never want you without your will. I am not an animal. Besides, I am a very loyal friend. What if those thugs had abducted and raped you? Can you imagine the danger you were in?"

Saloni looked at Arjun. His eyes were burning with anger. She decided that it was best to keep quiet for a while. She was happy to hear that he had unknowingly admitted to being in love with her. For now, she could live with that much. She couldn't get the images of him fighting for her out of her mind. He looked so macho! She was completely in love with him.

After a while, he fell asleep. Saloni was unable to sleep. She moved her hands to feel his strong arm and kissed his shoulder. She rested her head on his shoulder and went to sleep feeling safe and secure. Arjun was up early and decided to get down one stop before Orcha for safety. He awakened Saloni and they alighted from the bus. They went to a nearby motel and booked a room. The motel room was decent. They freshened up and ordered breakfast.

Arjun had calmed down by now. "Saloni, I am sorry about yesterday. But you have to trust me and my intentions. Promise me that you will never put yourself in danger again."

"I promise."

He looked away from her gaze.

"What is our next plan?" she asked.

"After lunch, we are going to walk to Orcha and hire a private car to Khajuraho. By now, the thugs would be aware that we are on our way to Khajuraho. So, the trick is to keep changing routes to reach there. I tried to call up Shiv yesterday. His phone was not reachable. He was not at the hotel too. I am worried about him. Were you able to talk to him yesterday?" he asked.

"Oh that? Er... no."

What a man! she thought. He admits to be in love with the woman he is escorting to meet her lover. She would have never been able to do that. It requires great courage to rip your heart and hand it to someone else to care for. It was unbelievable that such principled people exist in reality. She was never going to let go of him.

Arjun and Saloni set off half an hour after lunch for the seventeen-kilometre walk to Orcha. Saloni was looking forward to spend some solitary time with Arjun. The day was pleasant with a clear blue sky. The road was picturesque with hills and lakes on either side. Occasionally, they could see a few villages and old Rajput style marble houses with high arches and pillars. Very few vehicles passed their way, most took the highway parallel to this road.

Arjun was in a good mood.

"Do you work out?" asked Saloni.

"Isn't it evident?" questioned Arjun.

"Yes, it is from your toned abs and muscular arms, chest and legs," she said checking him out.

"You are very observant," replied Arjun amused by her gesture.

"Those were some karate chops you struck yesterday. Very impressive."

"That was Dim Mak martial arts."

"Why didn't you fight the thugs when they were kidnapping you? Not enough motivation huh?"

He smiled. "They threatened to kill Mr Sanyal. That was enough motivation to stay calm."

"Why are you so loyal to the Sanyals? Do you think they feel the same for you?"

"I don't care what they feel for me. They are the only family I have."

"Yesterday, in the bus, I had switched on your phone to check your messages, not to call Shiv."

"What messages?" he asked raising his eyebrows curiously.

"The messages you said you received from your female fans after your performances," she said, embarrassed.

"And?"

"I read those. Those girls were literally begging you to spend an evening or even an hour with them. How many did you respond to?" she asked flaring her nostrils.

"You didn't check the sent messages? I responded to all of them," he replied calmly.

"Oh! I missed checking those."

"Remind me to show you when I switch on my phone next time. For now, curb your curiosity."

"You are like Jason Statham from the Transporter series, except that you are more handsome," she said smiling at him.

"In what way?"

"You are a cool fighter, you are mysterious, you don't ask questions and you are cold, yet hot."

"Hollywood again," he muttered.

"You said something?"

"Nothing, I take that as a compliment. Thank you."

They walked admiring nature's beauty. They jogged intermittently. Finally, in about three hours, they reached Orcha. Arjun enquired and hired a car for Khajuraho.

"It will take close to three hours to reach Khajuraho," he informed Saloni.

"Alright, I am in no hurry," she replied.

He frowned and got into the car. He sat in front, leaving the backseat for Saloni to rest. Although Saloni clarified that she didn't need rest, Arjun insisted on sitting in the front.

She tried to pull him and said, "I want you to sit here, next to me."

"Don't make it difficult for me, Saloni," he said with saddened eyes and released himself from her grip.

The more he tried to distance himself from her, the more she wanted to be close to him. They stopped for a coffee break just before reaching Khajuraho. The restaurant was crowded with youngsters and foreigners. The place had great music and a dance floor. Saloni and Arjun were glad to be in a crowded place. It felt safe.

A young girl approached Arjun. "Hi handsome! Aren't you the dude who recently sang at the Orchids? I loved your performance. You are a rockstar! My name is Shaina," she said extending her hand.

Arjun stood up and courteously took her hand, "Pleasure meeting you, Shaina."

"Can I join you?" asked Shaina and pulled a chair without waiting for a reply.

"Arjun, the video of your performance has gone viral. You are a sensation. It's a pity you are not single anymore," she added.

"Excuse me?" said Arjun with raised eyebrows.

"Yeah, I received your reply yesterday stating your relationship status, 'Not single.'"

Arjun looked at Saloni suspiciously and said, "Oh! Did you? Well! That was a mistake. I am absolutely unattached currently."

Shaina looked at Saloni quizzically.

"Oh! She is just a friend. I am supervising her safe travel to Khajuraho. Don't be bothered by her," he said in order to tease Saloni.

Saloni was embarrassed and hurt.

"In that case, you don't mind a dance with me, right? Don't say no, please. It's my birthday."

"Oh! Happy birthday Shaina," said Arjun hugging Shaina and placing a light kiss on her cheek.

Saloni was flushed with anger and jealousy.

She stood up and grabbed Shaina, "Happy birthday dear. You look beautiful! May I have the pleasure of dancing with you first?"

Shaina and Arjun exchanged puzzled looks.

"Well! I am a lesbian," she added.

"Oh!" exclaimed Shaina. "Sure. I hope you don't mind a little waiting, Arjun."

Arjun rolled his eyes on hearing Saloni's explanation. "No problem. Go ahead and have a good time," he said.

Saloni danced with Shaina and gradually moved away from Arjun's sight. When they were out of his field of vision, Saloni grabbed Shaina and said, "Listen, if you don't back off, I am going to extract your eyeballs, pull your hair apart and bleed you from your nose."

"What! Are you crazy?"

"Yes, about him," she said staring at Shaina. "I mean every word of what I said. You are going to politely refuse to dance with Arjun. Understand?"

After the song, they went back to Arjun's table.

Arjun stood to take over, but Shaina hesitated, "Thank you, but I am overwhelmed after dancing with your friend. I want to linger in the moment." She left in a hurry. Arjun was confused.

He asked Saloni, "What did you tell her?"

"Me?" asked Saloni innocently.

Arjun sighed and they left the place.

Saloni and Arjun reached Khajuraho International Hotel at about 9 p.m. Arjun had tried calling up Shiv at the hotel on numerous occasions in the past two days. The only important information he learnt was that Shiv was staying in room number 101 on the first floor. Arjun and Saloni decided to go directly to Shiv's room using the fire exit. That way, they could dodge any thugs waiting for them at the reception.

The reception of the hotel was crowded by guests who were collecting their room keys after returning from the light and sound show at Kandariya Mahadev Temple. Taking advantage of the situation, Saloni and Arjun escaped into the fire exit unnoticed. Room number 101 was at the end of the corridor. Saloni knocked on the door and realized that it wasn't locked.

Saloni pushed open the door. Shiv was sitting on a chair next to his bed. He looked devastated. His eyes were red from lack of sleep, his hair was scattered and his stubble had turned into a light beard. Arjun and Saloni had never seen him so shattered.

Shiv looked up at the door. He got up from his chair and began moving fast towards them. Saloni feared that Shiv was going to punch Arjun due to the power of attorney misunderstanding.

She stood in between them. "No Shiv, Arjun is innocent. He signed the documents to save your dad."

Shiv gently moved Saloni out of the way and hugged Arjun. Both Arjun and Saloni were surprised. This behaviour was unexpected.

Shiv said in a choked voice, "They have taken away Mohini."

"Mohini?" asked Saloni. "I thought he was with Nysa," she said looking at Arjun.

Arjun took his distraught friend inside and made him sit on the bed. "What are you talking about?"

"I can't do it alone," said Shiv.

"Are you not mad at me?" asked Arjun.

"I was, but later, I was convinced that you couldn't harm dad or me," replied Shiv.

Arjun smiled and looked contended and elated by the trust his friend had placed in him.

Saloni raised her eyebrows and gave Arjun a thumbs-up sign. "The love is mutual then, huh?"

Arjun ignored Saloni's comment. "Who is Mohini? Were you with two women in Khajuraho? Where is Nysa?"

"What are you saying? Nysa is Mohini," replied Shiv.

"Oh! So, Nysa isn't her actual name?"

"No, it is her actual name, Abhay," replied Shiv.

"Wait a minute, who is Abhay?" asked Arjun, looking confused.

"You," replied Shiv.

Saloni pulled Arjun away, "I think he is in shock after Nysa's kidnapping. He needs therapy."

"I don't need therapy, Pallavi," shouted Shiv.

She said, "Oh, wonderful! Now I have a new name too!"

Arjun came back to Shiv and said, "It's going to be alright. We will find Nysa … I mean Mohini. You were not at the hotel yesterday?"

"I went to find clues at the hospital from where she was kidnapped. Then, I went to the police station. No leads anywhere," he said looking pitiful.

While they were talking, the intercom rang. Arjun picked up the phone.

Tony spoke fast in a tensed voice, "Shiv sir, Tony here. Some armed thugs are coming up to your room. I have put up a staircase in your balcony. My man is waiting in a red Scorpio near the back gate of the hotel. Come down, quick."

Arjun put down the phone receiver, secured the door and scanned the place. He picked up Shiv's personal belongings and rushed Shiv and Saloni to the balcony. "We have to move fast. The thugs are here for us."

Shiv refused to move. "I have to face them. They may have news on Nysa."

"We are not sure if they are the same thugs who kidnapped Nysa. We have a group of thugs trailing us too," said Arjun. "For now, we have to flee."

"Huh?" asked Shiv looking perplexed.

Arjun ushered him to the balcony. They heard loud banging on the door. All of them were down the staircase in less than a minute. Tony was waiting for them downstairs. He led them to the waiting Scorpio. Soon, they were on the highway to Panna National Park. "Where are we off to?" asked Arjun.

"To the miner's village. It is the safest place for us right now," replied Tony.

"You could never really move out of that village, huh Aamir?" Shiv asked Tony.

Tony had a puzzled look on his face.

"Let me guess," interrupted Saloni. "Aamir isn't your actual name."

Tony nodded.

"Do you mind explaining why you are on a renaming spree?" Saloni asked Shiv.

Shiv was staring down at the floor of the car. He didn't hear Saloni. Once at the village, Arjun put Shiv to sleep.

"How come I don't get to see this side of your personality?" asked Saloni.

"Well, you haven't earned it yet," replied Arjun.

"I am trying hard."

"You are confused about what you want."

"I was. I am clear now," she said gazing at Arjun.

Tony was listening to the exchange of conversation between Saloni and Arjun.

"You too are on your way," he said to Arjun.

"Way to where?" asked Arjun.

"Way to lunacy, like Shiv sir. He too showed similar signs after he met Nysa madam," replied Tony.

"You have no family?" asked Saloni.

"My parents don't live with me. I am single. Most villagers here are distantly related to each other. That's why, this is a safe place. No one dares to mess with me here. This is my fortress," said Tony proudly.

Shiv was feeling better after he got up from sleep. All of them had breakfast.

Arjun started the conversation, "I hope Mr Sanyal is fine."

"Oh yes, he is. I called up Saloni's dad yesterday. He has taken him to his house for better care," said Shiv.

"We have to find Nysa," added Shiv looking harrowed.

"Wait, we need to understand what has happened here. Time for some exchange of information," said Arjun. "Let everyone share their side of the story to get the complete picture."

They spent the next couple of hours doing that.

"So, that means, somebody invaded Sanyal House and kidnapped Arjun in Mumbai. At about the same time, somebody tried to shoot me and kidnapped Nysa in Khajuraho. However, we are not sure if the same group of brutes is behind all this. We don't know what they want and how to find Nysa," summarized Shiv.

"Yes, and from what you told us about your dream, you think we are all associated from past lives. You get to play the good guy in both lives, I am a bad guy turned good guy who has deceived Pallavi, and Tony is stalked by a black cobra from his past life. Now, that could just be a story generated by your brain trying to link up stuff," concluded Arjun.

"Wait, there's more. Arjun was Abhay, Tony was Aamir, Nysa was Mohini, you were Rudra, and I was Pallavi, right?" added Saloni.

"That explains the origin of our new names. I kind of like the part of the story where Abhay repents and leaps to his death to meet Pallavi. That's so romantic!"

"You are finding this funny? You guys don't believe me? All this is too much of a coincidence to be ignored," said Shiv.

"Alright," said Arjun looking at his distraught friend. "I totally believe you, Shiv. Right now, our priority is to retrieve Nysa from the kidnappers. Have they contacted you?"

"No," replied Shiv.

"Then, we have to wait until they contact us for ransom or for whatever they want. Let's hope that it was not Nysa they were after. In that case, they already have what they wanted."

Shiv looked up at the ceiling in distress and said, "I hope not."

Saloni looked at Arjun with wide eyes and whispered, "You believe his story?"

Arjun whispered back, "Sshh! Just look at his state. He is a mess." He addressed the others and said, "Let's chalk out a plan."

For the next few minutes, they tried to discuss ways to find Nysa. However, they were at a loss.

"With no clues at the hospital and police station, where do we start looking for her?" asked Arjun.

"I think Mittal is behind all this. We should keep track of his movements," said Shiv.

"You could be right. I just remembered that Synchron Technologies is one of his business ventures," added Arjun.

"I have sent my men to find if any local goons were involved in the kidnapping," informed Tony.

"Why are you helping us out? What have you got to gain?" asked Saloni suspiciously looking at Tony.

"Shiv sir saved my life. I owe him. And from his story, he saved me in my past life too," replied Tony.

They decided to wait for news from Tony's men before proceeding further.

Saloni caught a private moment with Arjun and asked, "You really believe Shiv's dream?"

"I don't want to," replied a dejected looking Arjun. "But if what he says is true, I deserve to be crucified. No amount of repentance is going to wash away what I did to you."

Saloni smiled. "Well, today is your lucky day. Here's your chance to redeem yourself," she said opening her arms for a hug.

Arjun moved close to Saloni, put down her arms and said, "Right now, you are smitten like most of the crazy girls who message me. I have seen this kind of behaviour before. Talk to me when you are over this and when your mind is clear."

Saloni walked away smirking.

Shiv was lost in thoughts. Arjun sat next to Shiv, put his arm around his shoulder and said, "I have never seen you so beaten down. Don't worry, we will find her."

Tears welled up in Shiv's eyes. "She almost gave her life for me. I don't think I will survive without her."

"You have to, if you want to find her. How about that pack of cigarettes I am saving for you? You want it now?" joked Arjun.

"I can see that you don't need it anymore," chuckled Shiv, momentarily taking his mind off the situation.

"I may. Right now, she is confused whether she is infatuated with me or was infatuated with you in the past. The wait is killing me," said Arjun.

Saloni was sitting in the veranda and admiring the village.

Shiv sat next to her and placed his hand around her shoulder, "Sweetheart, I missed you."

Saloni smiled.

"Just a smile, no 'missed you too'?" asked Shiv.

"You know, you were right," he added.

"About what?" asked Saloni.

"You always said that I would realize someday that you were the one for me."

"What! What about Nysa?" Saloni turned to face him.

"I have to get her released because I feel guilty about her kidnapping. It's guilt, not love. You are my true love. You always wanted me to make love to you. Now, I think I am ready."

She released herself from his hold and moved away, "Shiv, I know I have led you on, but I was confused. I never loved you, just felt indebted to you."

"Doesn't matter. I love you," he said trying to kiss her.

Saloni pushed Shiv away. "Can't you understand what I am saying?" she screamed.

Arjun came running into the veranda on hearing the commotion, "What's going on? Are you alright, Saloni? Shiv?"

"We are fine pal. I just won that entire pack of cigarettes. You are not going to need it. There's no more confusion," he said winking and feeling happy for Arjun.

Saloni looked angrily at Shiv and asked, "What if I wouldn't have resisted? Would you have …"

"No! Never," Shiv cut her short.

"Happy? Need more proof?" she said to Arjun scornfully.

Arjun was hurt. He tried to explain, "Shiv was on his own in this."

She didn't wait to hear. Arjun walked towards Shiv and punched him. Shiv was caught off guard. Arjun had never reacted like this before. He recovered from the punch, looked at Arjun and chuckled.

"What? Have you lost your mind?" Arjun asked throwing up his hands in the air.

Shiv moved close to Arjun. "I know you are very happy in there," he said pointing at Arjun's heart.

Arjun looked at Shiv and was unable to remain angry. He too began laughing. The two punched each other lightly and hugged.

Arjun gave the pack of cigarettes to Shiv who tossed it into a bin in the veranda.

Tony's men returned with some vital information. Tony came back and picked up his gun.

Arjun interrupted, "What's the matter? Who are those men?"

"They are my men. The kidnappers tried to contact Shiv at the hotel and through his phone, but for obvious reasons were unable to. One of the kidnappers is waiting at the village outskirts with a message. He refuses to hand it to anyone other than Shiv. I am going to get the message. He was scared to come into the village because he may not be able to go back alive."

Shiv heard what Tony said. He resisted Tony from going. "I will go and meet him. I don't want anything to go wrong."

"You are not going alone. I am accompanying you," replied Arjun.

Shiv snatched the gun from Tony and pointed it towards himself, "If any of you follow me, I will shoot myself. Without her, I am dead anyway."

Everyone backed off. Shiv left after taking directions from Tony's men. Tony and Arjun followed him from a safe distance. Shiv met the kidnapper's goon. He was wearing a mask. He handed over a packet to Shiv and fled. As soon as he left, Arjun and Tony joined Shiv.

Shiv glanced at both of them and said, "I knew you wouldn't be far away."

They rushed to Tony's house with the packet.

Shiv opened the packet with trembling hands. It had a pen drive and a folded paper. Tony arranged for a laptop. The pen drive had a video showing a dimly lighted room. In the room, Nysa was bound to a chair and had duct tape covering her mouth. Her shoulder was freshly bandaged. She wasn't wearing hospital clothes.

A man appeared from behind with a gun pointed at Nysa's temple. He pulled off the duct tape from over her mouth. Shiv felt Nysa's pain when he heard the ripping sound of the duct tape. The camera focused on a close shot of Nysa's face. She was in tears. The man poked the gun in her shoulder wound, which began to bleed. Shiv was unable to watch the torture and closed his eyes. She silently winced in pain.

She said, "Shiv, if you are watching this, I want you to know that I love you. I didn't want any of this to happen to us. I was hoping to spend my life with you. You don't have to do whatever these people want. I will always love you, no matter ..."

Before she could say anymore, the gunman hit the butt of his gun on her back. She wept and shrieked in pain. Shiv had a sense of déjà vu and was unable to watch anymore. He got up, went to the window and punched into the window pane. The glass broke with a shattering sound. Arjun and Saloni rushed towards Shiv. Tony paused the video and joined the rest of them. Shiv's hand was bleeding. Arjun bandaged his hand and made him sit.

"I know you are not okay. But, if you lose your cool, how will we find Nysa?" said Arjun.

Shiv nodded and they continued watching the video.

The masked man reappeared, "Shiv, listen carefully. I have sent you a picture of an ancient artwork in the packet. Your dad owns it. You have to hand it over to me in exchange for your girlfriend. In case you feel she is not enough motivation, I want you to see this."

The video showed another room where Mr Sanyal and Mr Ballad were held captive. Mr Sanyal was lying on a bed with an oxygen mask fixed over his nose and mouth. A terrified nurse was standing by his side. Mr Ballad was bound to a chair.

The man reappeared on the camera, "I will provide good medical care for your dad and girlfriend, as long as you behave yourself. I assume you are smart enough to not involve the police. I will get in touch with you tomorrow."

The video went blank after this. Shiv unfolded the paper. It had a picture of a rectangular sculpture that was divided into four parts. On each part, an ancient temple was sculpted. Out of the four temples, Shiv could only identify the Kandariya Mahadev Temple of Khajuraho in one of the parts. Cobras were depicted in front of each temple. The fourth temple at the right hand lower corner of the sculpture showed a pair of parallel wavy lines. Shiv had never seen the sculpture in his dad's collection.

He looked up from the paper, "They have been kidnapped for this artwork? Is it so valuable? I have never seen it before."

Arjun looked at the paper and passed it on to Tony. Saloni was weeping bitterly. Arjun sat by her side and held her hands to console her.

He wiped her tears, "It's going to be fine."

Shiv comforted Saloni, "I am sorry. You are all paying the price of being close to me. I will get your dad out of this, I promise."

Saloni nodded. "Not your fault."

Tony had a good look at the paper. He got up and picked up a book from his collection. He opened a page showing the same sculpture.

"This sculpture belonged to the Khajuraho museum for a long time. I am not sure how it has landed with Mr Sanyal. Not much is mentioned in this book about the sculpture. We may have to find an expert on Khajuraho history and sculptures who could help," he said.

He passed on the book to each one of them. Saloni scanned the book to identify the author. It was Anish Kapoor. She showed it to Shiv. Shiv knew what he had to do.

He called up Anish Kapoor from Tony's landline, hoping that it was not bugged or tracked, "Hello sir, Shiv Sanyal here. I called to apologize for the other day. On your advice, I have spent quite a few days in Khajuraho and am studying the sculptures. Sir, I am impressed by your impeccable knowledge about Khajuraho. Yes sir … hmm … sure sir. I do have a question. It is about a sculpture I read about in one of your books. I am mailing you the picture right now... Okay sir... No problem. Thank you."

All the others were waiting for Shiv to explain. "We have to wait for a couple of hours."

Arjun immediately emailed the picture to Anish Kapoor.

He said, "On my email, I have inventories of the items kept in Mr Sanyal's various lockers. None of them mentions the sculpture."

He passed the laptop to Shiv to have a look.

Shiv said, "Where do we look for it?"

He got up and stood staring vacantly outside the window. Saloni had gone back to the veranda and Arjun followed her. Tony decided to visit the museum to find out more.

Arjun sat beside Saloni, held her hand and asked, "Do you trust me?"

"More than my life," she replied looking at him.

"Then leave everything to me, I'll take care of it."

She rested her head on his strong shoulders, took a deep breath and closed her eyes. Arjun sat beside her, comforting her for a long time. Shiv was constantly checking his emails for a reply from Anish Kapoor. Finally, after a little more than two hours, Anish Kapoor replied. Shiv called out to Arjun.

Hi Shiv,

I am impressed by your modesty. The sculpture in question is owned by your dad. I am surprised that you did not mention it. Anyway, the sculpture belonged to Khajuraho museum for a long time until a descendant of King Vidyadhara's family staked legal claim.

After a long legal battle, the sculpture was handed over to the family. Your dad bought the sculpture for ten crore rupees from a charity exhibition held by the family. This was about eight years ago. There are no reports of any further sale of this piece by your dad.

The sculpture depicts the golden era of art in the three powerful dynasties of the 10th century, namely, the Western Chalukya, Chola and Chandela. The three identifiable temples are Kalleshwara Temple, Brihadisvara Temple and Kandariya Mahadev Temple, belonging to the three dynasties, respectively. The fourth temple depicted in the right hand lower corner has not been identified.

Some interesting stories are associated with the sculpture. The three dynasties were constantly at war with each other. There was a time when all of them were under threat from the infamous invader Mahmud of Ghazni.

Although at war, the three kings were united in their fight against a foreign invader. To ensure that none amongst the three turned traitor, they signed a pact of unity against foreign invaders. To guarantee their commitment to the pact, all the three kingdoms put together valuables, gold coins, precious stones, sculptures and scriptures from their kingdoms as assurance of funding to raise an army against Mahmud of Ghazni. This treasure amounting to thousands of crores in today's era was hidden at the fourth location depicted in the picture. The funds were never used because a common army was never raised, which means the treasure is just lying somewhere waiting to be discovered.

The cobras depicted at the gate of each temple were considered as protectors of the treasure. The story is that snake charmers from Chandela kingdom had mastered the art of training cobras to attack enemies. The cobras were trained using the conditioned reflex method to identify the smell of their enemies. Prisoners of earlier wars with Mahmud of Ghazni were used as baits for the training. These snakes were left to infest the treasure site to protect it from foreign invaders, especially Mahmud of Ghazni. The mutational genetic changes caused by the conditioned reflex were expected to be passed on from generation to generation of these trained cobras. Funny and unbelievable, isn't it?'

Shiv and Arjun looked at each other. They now knew why a black cobra was always stalking Tony. They read further:

'The location of the fourth temple was a secret that was well kept by all the three dynasties. Later, all the three dynasties were attacked and ruled by the Mughal dynasty. The story of the treasure was lost in the sculpture. Not sure if any of this is true.

I hope this helps.

"So, it is the treasure they are after," concluded Arjun.

"What if they don't release our people after we hand over the sculpture?" questioned Shiv.

"We do not even know where the sculpture is," added Saloni.

In the meanwhile, Tony returned from the museum. He read the email and was shocked.

"The cobras have been trained to attack me? I am a descendent of the tribe of Mahmud of Ghazni in this life too? There is no relief from them then."

Shiv went to Tony and hugged him, "I trust you. You are a good man."

Tony hugged him back and said, "How do I let the snakes know that?"

Tony continued, "I went to the museum to meet an expert. He is a close friend. The story given by him is the same as in the email. Only the snake part was unknown to him. He said that Hindu temples often depicted animals as protectors of temple entrances, and snakes were considered sacred back then. Also, he said that these parallel wavy lines in the fourth part depicted a river. In those days, rivers were often depicted in this manner."

"Okay, let's concentrate. We need to find where the sculpture is," reminded Saloni.

"The only person who knows about it is Mr Sanyal. However, there is no way of contacting him. The kidnappers may have already questioned him, but due to his ill health, he may have been of no help. So, they must have decided to kidnap him to force Shiv to find the sculpture," analyzed Arjun.

"Let's take a break to process this. My brain is a wreck," said Shiv.

"I need coffee," said Saloni.

"I only have beer in my house," replied Tony. "But we can go to the corner stall for tea."

"No, that place is not suitable for Saloni," replied Shiv.

"I know a good place about fifteen minutes from here," said Arjun.

Saloni knew he was talking about the café she had visited with Arjun. Although hesitant, she joined them.

All of them settled at a corner table in the coffee shop. Shiv borrowed a paper and pen from a waiter and began scribbling something. Saloni excused herself to freshen up. Arjun went to place the order.

At the table, Shiv was waiting for the others to join him. He placed the paper on the table.

"All of you take a look," he said.

Each one of them looked at the paper and passed it on until it reached Shiv again.

Chandela Kandariya Mahadev Temple Snake	Chola Brihadisvara Temple Snake
Western Chalukya Kalleshwara Temple Snake	River? Temple? Snake

"This is the information we have. Any suggestions on what could be in the last box?" asked Shiv.

"I am no expert in history, but if there is a Western Chalukya, wouldn't there be an Eastern Chalukya as well?" asked Arjun.

"Brilliant!" overreacted Saloni.

The others looked at her with a smirk.

"There was an Eastern Chalukya in those days. It had friendly ties with the Cholas. The pact could have been signed in their territory and the treasure could have been hidden there," added Shiv.

"The kingdom must have been huge. Is it possible to scrutinize and locate one temple in such a huge place?" asked Tony.

"We could google for images of ancient temples near river banks in the Eastern Chalukya territory and see if any of them match our sculpture," said Saloni with excitement.

Tony opened his laptop and handed it over to Saloni. She surfed for a long time trying several keywords, but found no match.

Finally, she gave up and looked dejected. "No luck. We are stuck again. We do not have the sculpture and there's no clue to find the treasure."

"We have to find a solution by tomorrow, before the kidnappers contact us again," said Shiv.

They sipped their coffee and ate sandwiches.

After a while of thinking and getting nowhere, Shiv said, "I think I know who could help us."

Everyone else looked at him expectantly.

"Devi ji," he replied.

They got up and went back to Tony's house.

Shiv called up Devi, "Hello Ma'am." He waited to hear what she said and continued, "No ma'am. Not only Nysa, but Mr Ballad and dad too are in danger. It's about a sculpture from King Vidyadhara's family that probably leads to a treasure." He listened again. "Dad had showed it you? No ma'am, I have never seen it around … Hmm … okay … I'll do that. Thank you. I knew you could help."

The others waited for Shiv to explain.

This is what she said, "In that era, kings knew that such information would be passed on from generation to generation. They didn't rely on verbal passage of information due to fear of loss of vital facts. Nothing on the sculpture, except for ageing artefacts, is without purpose. She asked me to look carefully. She asked me to bargain smartly with the enemy. She strangely added, 'Not all plans see completion.'"

Tony got up to get the Khajuraho museum book. He inspected the picture to have a good look. He didn't notice anything new and passed on the book for the others to see.

Shiv looked at the picture carefully, "Look! There is a line in all the three parts. Initially, I mistook these lines for artefacts, but they are too identical to be ignored. Also, there are three lines in the part with the unknown temple. This surely isn't an artifact!" exclaimed Shiv.

"Which means that we need to collect something from each of these temples, maybe clues, to find the unknown temple," added Arjun.

"Okay, so when the kidnappers contact us, we have to convince them to let us find the treasure because we do not have the sculpture. They get thousands of crores instead of only ten crores. That sounds like an attractive deal," said Saloni.

All of them agreed and called it a day. Saloni slept in the bedroom and the rest of them relaxed in the living room. Shiv was unable to sleep and went to relax in the veranda.

Tony was already helping himself to generous amounts of whisky in the veranda. "Want some?" he offered.

Shiv declined. Arjun joined Shiv and Tony in the veranda. Arjun was soon lying on his back with his arms below his head and gazing at the stars above.

"What are you thinking about?" asked Shiv.

"Just wondering why you love Nysa so much. You have hardly known her for a couple of days. What could be the basis of such love?" asked Arjun.

"I have known her for several lifetimes, Arjun, just like I have known you. What is the basis of your friendship and loyalty? You have had several occasions to take over Sanyal Empire, but not once did the thought cross your mind. Our feelings of hate, love, like and dislike for strangers may not be completely without basis, you know," explained Shiv lying beside Arjun.

"Man, I don't know what you two are talking about, but I love you both," said Tony and lay down beside them.

All three fell asleep gazing at the stars.

In the morning, Saloni checked on them to find them snuggled and sleeping in the veranda.

"And they say they are not gay," she said rolling her eyes.

Tony's men brought some coffee and breakfast for all of them.

Shiv was anxious. "How will they contact us? Will they call on Tony's landline?"

"I know that they won't dare to come here personally," said Tony.

"Let's wait and watch," said Arjun.

At noon, one of Tony's men came rushing into the house, "Boss, a masked man wants to meet Shiv sir. He is outside the village. Should I get him?"

Tony nodded giving permission. In about fifteen minutes, a masked man stood in front of them.

He was nervous. "If you touch me, all of them will be killed," he said shifting his weight from one leg to another.

"Chill! We are not stupid to harm you," replied Shiv.

The masked man said, "My boss will call on my cell phone to speak to you."

"Smart. He doesn't want to risk being tracked, huh?" asked Arjun.

"We could still track his location by finding the active cell phone in this house," whispered Saloni.

"Hollywood?" Arjun whispered back.

"Boss is smart. He is calling from a different location with an untraceable number," replied the kidnapper.

"Hmm … hear that?" Arjun said to Saloni.

In a few seconds, the masked man's phone rang. He handed the phone to Shiv. He put the call on speaker. He explained the situation as best as he could, hoping to convince the kidnapper to let them find the treasure. The kidnapper said that he needed a few minutes to think. All of them waited anxiously.

Tony said, "This is the voice that used to call me for information about you. He was the one who paid me to shoot you."

"Hmm. Not surprising," said Shiv.

"This isn't his original voice, he is obviously using a voice modifier," said Saloni.

"But isn't the tone familiar?" asked Arjun.

"Not sure, can't place it," said Shiv.

The phone rang again. The kidnapper agreed to let them find the treasure. However, he said that his men would accompany them in the task. In return, Shiv bargained and asked the kidnapper to promise the release of Mr Sanyal and Mr Ballad after they would find three clues. The kidnapper agreed and added that he would send a surprise gift for Shiv. Shiv was scared and hoped he hadn't pissed off the kidnapper by asking for too much. The kidnapper ordered them to start next morning after his men joined them.

"I will direct my men to follow us at a safe distance," said Tony after the masked man left.

"I don't think that is a good idea. We don't want to rub this kidnapper the wrong way. A lot is at stake," said Shiv.

"You are right. He is always going to have an upper hand. For now, let's play his game," said Arjun.

"I second that," added Saloni.

The next morning, they were all up early. Shiv was taking a shower lost in deep thoughts. He hoped that his dad, Mr Ballad and Nysa were fine. Suddenly, there was a knock on his bathroom door.

He knew from the knock that it was Arjun. "Wrong door pal, Saloni is probably in the other bathroom."

Arjun shouted, "Shiv, you have to see this now."

Shiv got worried. He turned off the shower, wrapped a towel around his waist and came out with drenched body and hair. Nysa was standing in the room. Arjun was standing near the bathroom and smiling.

"Is this a dream?" he whispered.

"Check it out yourself," replied Arjun and left the room.

Nysa swayed a little as though she was giddy. Shiv rushed to support her.

"You alright?" he asked in a soft and husky voice.

"How can I be? Look at you, sexy and tanned with a skimpy towel around your bare and wet body. Your hair all wet and gelled back. What do you expect?" she replied trying to regain her posture.

He chuckled and began incessantly kissing her face, lips and neck when there was an interruption, "Shiv, I am a man of my words. Did you like the surprise? Now, if you are done with the cuddling and kissing, let's get back to business."

Shiv began looking around for the source of the voice. Nysa showed him a gadget wrapped around her right wrist.

The voice spoke again from her gadget, "All of you come together in ten minutes. We have business to discuss."

Shiv observed Nysa. She looked pale, had mild undereye dark circles and had lost weight. He felt sorry for her. He kissed her on her bandaged shoulder wound and let her go. All of them assembled in the living room. Five men from the kidnapper's gang soon joined them.

Tony's men had been instructed to let them in without probing and frisking. They were decently dressed in semiformal checker shirts and formal trousers to mingle with a decent looking crowd.

The kidnapper spoke through Nysa's gadget, "All of you extend your right hands. My men will fix similar gadgets on your wrists. Through the gadget, I'll be able to track and communicate with each one of you. If you try to run away farther than five kilometres from me or tamper with the gadget, an alarm will be set off and the gadget will explode on your body with obvious consequences. Even within five kilometres, I can trigger the explosion immediately or by setting a timer. So, there is no way to escape. After the job is done, I'll take off the gadget and set you free. Do not forget that Sanyal and Ballad are with me and you are just a click away from your death."

"I have seen this in a movie," said a shocked looking Saloni.

"Freerunner," replied Arjun.

"Yes! These gadgets are remote controlled, meaning our kidnapper is within a certain radius of us," she added.

The gang members fixed fiber gadgets that looked like digital watches on everyone's wrists. A green light flickered on the strap.

"These goons are not the ones who had kidnapped me. Either the gang is huge or there are two gangs targeting us," said Arjun.

Shiv nodded.

This time, the kidnapper spoke through Shiv's gadget, "Kandariya Mahadev Temple will be your first target to find your clue."

The thugs checked all of them for weapons. Tony was asked to hand over his gun. Arjun punched one of the thugs who was misbehaving with Saloni and trying to grope her on the pretext of frisking her.

"Easy tiger," said the kidnapper's voice.

The kidnapper spoke to his men, "Focus on the mission, not the miss. Understand?"

Shiv spoke to Tony, "You need not join us. It's too risky."

"I have given you my word. Besides, I owe you my life," replied Tony.

"You owe me nothing," said Shiv.

The voice interrupted through Shiv's gadget, "It's not your call any longer. Tony knows too much to be left here unsupervised. He has no choice but to accompany you."

*O*n the outskirts of Tony's village was an ordinary-looking man in his early fifties seated in an inexpensive old car following all the GPS trackers on the wrists of his victims. His laptop screen displayed the movement of the people under his control. The feeling of being able to control rich people gave him a high. Their fear gave him an adrenaline rush. He had held Mr Ballad and Mr Sanyal captive in Mumbai, fiercely guarded by his men. Finally, he was going to earn thousands of crores and would join the league of the rich and famous.

He was tired of small robberies and frauds. He wished to give up everything and settle down, own a luxurious villa, a beautiful trophy wife and lots of money to splurge.

A few murders that he had committed at the beginning of his fraudulent career had been long forgotten and lost in the list of unsolved crimes. He had been lucky to zero in on rich people with no heirs and hence, no pursuers of their murder cases.

One of his victims, a rich couple, owned many rare artworks that he had sold at rather cheap prices. However, by now, he had good knowledge of the worth of these artworks. He knew how the network operated. He knew when and where to find the right buyer. He had mastered the trade.

Sanyal and his son were ideal targets. If both died, no one would bother. Sanyal bought rare artworks for charity and his son didn't care about money. After he found the treasure, he could keep Saloni or

Nysa as his mistress. Or perhaps, he could have them both. He smiled at the thought.

He had watched both the girls closely. Saloni was like a doll, delicate and pretty. Nysa had a dusky complexion, luscious lips, full body and heavy breasts. She was a sex siren. The beauty spot on her slender neck turned him on. He brought her along to Khajuraho because he didn't trust his men to keep their hands off her. He would be able to watch her here.

He was mesmerized by the lifestyle of the rich and famous and had decided to become one of them. His dead parents would be so proud of him. They would finally realize that the expensive education they provided him was not in vain. He wanted to work independently, but his parents forced him to work with one of their employers. He obliged until they were alive. After that, he was free. It didn't matter that he had to earn his freedom. A little arsenic in his parent's food had put them to rest forever. After all, they had struggled for so long. The rest was well deserved.

He looked at the screen. The rich gang was moving in search of the treasure. He ordered his driver to follow the route to Kandariya Mahadev Temple.

It was a good thing that the wrist gadget was made up of sturdy fiber-reinforced plastic, and would easily pass undetected through metal detectors at the temple. He tapped his shirt pocket to check if the remote was in place. The gadget seller had told him that the device worked only within a radius of five kilometres. He could press the red button on the remote and the device would explode. He could also set a timer and enjoy a little play time watching his victims suffer as they moved closer to death with each tick of the timer. The device would go out of range outside the five-kilometre radius. He would not have any control on the device beyond that range. But he had lied to his captives that it would explode if they moved out of the radius. So, he was in total control now. It would keep them in check.

He wondered what was fitted in such a small gadget that could cause an explosion big enough to kill a person. Some inventions are like boons, he thought.

Outside the temple, the gang members warned Shiv and others against acting suspicious or asking for help. The thugs handed them three cameras, one each to Shiv, Arjun and Tony, and waited outside the temple gate. Shiv, Arjun, Tony, Saloni and Nysa, gathered in the temple courtyard.

"What are we looking for?" asked Tony.

All of them looked at Shiv.

"I don't know. Let's observe anything that looks odd and meet here in two hours to discuss," said Shiv.

"Everything looks odd to me," said Saloni looking around.

"Everything is too familiar to me," said Tony adjusting his Khajuraho stole around his neck.

"Alright, disperse and get to work," commanded the kidnapper's voice through Saloni's gadget.

Arjun held Saloni's hand and moved in one direction. Shiv and Nysa moved in another. Tony kept wondering about whom to join. He finally decided to wait near the temple steps till they finished inspecting the exterior.

They started from the gate and the temple compound. They clicked several photographs of each other to appear like tourists. They touched and tapped whatever they felt had storage space. They tapped the concrete floor and scanned the outside premises of the temple. Finally, all four of them gathered at the gate of the temple building.

Tony was sitting on the steps leading to the temple interior. "Tony, you are guiding yourself today? No tourists?" asked one of the temple caretakers.

"My tourists wanted to explore on their own. Here they come," he said pointing at Arjun, Saloni, Shiv and Nysa.

"Oh! Honeymooning couples, huh?" asked the temple caretaker looking at them.

"Yes, looking for some excitement," replied Tony, winking at the caretaker.

"Let me take you through the history of these sculptures," said Tony to the four and got up to accompany them.

"Any luck?" asked Arjun.

Shiv shook his head in despair.

"Let's walk on the platform and check the sculptures on the outer wall of temple carefully. You two go from the other side," Saloni said to Shiv and Nysa.

Nysa was looking at the sculptures very observantly. For a moment, Shiv felt that Nysa remembered everything, but in the next, he felt that she was lost. Saloni was gawking at all the erotic sculptures on the outer wall of the temple.

"According to Shiv's dream, you have experienced all these positions. I'd like to experience the one with the headstand," she said winking at Arjun.

Arjun was looking at the sculptures with doleful eyes.

"I am not particularly proud of what I did to you back then. If everything is true, I hope you can forgive me someday. I'll make it up to you, I promise."

"I'll make sure you do," she replied moving a finger over his cheeks and lips.

They continued to click photographs and scan the place. Halfway at the back of the temple platform, the two couples met again. Neither of them had noticed anything unusual. They went back to the main entrance of the temple. They scanned the entrance and found nothing. They entered inside. The womb of the temple had a *Shivalinga*. All of them folded their hands and bowed their heads, asking for blessings, and then continued their search. The donation box was huge and had a see-through grill. Nothing, except money, was there.

They looked at the sculptures on the inner wall of the temple. It was dark in there. They had to strain their eyes to see. They tried to feel the sculptures to find lose stones or hidden spaces. They clicked photographs inside using the camera flash.

While Shiv was clicking one such photograph, the temple caretaker came inside and shouted, "No photography inside please! Tony, haven't you told your guests?"

They apologized and continued looking around. They tapped the pillars and found nothing unusual. At the end of two hours, they were dejected and gave up. They gathered outside the temple. Then, they went behind the temple and sat on the ground.

"Any luck?" asked the voice through Arjun's gadget.

"We are trying," replied Arjun.

"You just have today," warned the voice.

Shiv sat with his face buried in his hands. Nysa tried to comfort him by gently patting his back. She took the camera from him and saw the photographs. She went through all the photographs trying to find something unusual. The last photograph taken inside the temple was blurry because Shiv had moved the camera when the temple caretaker shouted.

Nysa asked Shiv, "Should I delete this one?"

Shiv took the camera from her and looked at the picture. It was fuzzy. He was about to delete it when he noticed something unusual at the top end of the frame—a circular form. He looked carefully by zooming in at that point. It looked like a picture of the sun. Or was it a logo, or an inscription? He showed the picture to the others. They all went back inside the temple to check.

They located the sculpture they were looking for. Tony looked around to check if the caretaker was around. He switched on his camera flashlight and focused on the sculpture. It was an inscription. It did not match the theme of the other carvings in the temple. It seemed like a misfit. It was at a height of eight feet, so none of them were able to touch and inspect it. The two girls decided to guard the passage, while Shiv climbed on Arjun's back to check.

Shiv inspected the inscription closely. The center of the sculpture had a small knob. It appeared like a chest that could be pulled out. Shiv tried to pull it out. It moved a little and then got stuck. Shiv stuck his hands in the little slit that had opened. He felt something inside but could not bring it out without completely opening the chest. Nysa came back to warn them about a group of tourists that was coming in. Shiv quickly pushed back the sculpture and got down.

They rushed outside.

"It will be impossible during the day to open that chest without being noticed," said Tony.

"So, what do we do?" asked Shiv wiping the sweat collected on his forehead.

"We come back at night for the light show. We will stay back and then retrieve whatever is inside," said Tony.

"Will the kidnapper agree?" asked Arjun.

"We have to convince him," replied Shiv.

The kidnapper readily agreed.

Shiv and Arjun sneaked inside the temple during the light and sound show in the evening and stayed back. Tony accompanied the girls to the car. They all waited in the car. Shiv had brought in some oil in a small bottle to smoothly open the chest. He poured some oil through the crevice and pulled hard. This time, the chest opened and Shiv removed the contents and carefully closed the chest.

Shiv and Arjun quickly moved outside to mingle with the crowd moving towards the exit. Tony, the girls and the thugs were surprised that Shiv and Arjun had returned so quickly. They all went back to Tony's house. The kidnapper smiled wickedly on learning about the development, and his car followed them at a safe distance.

At Tony's house, Shiv removed the contents that were tucked in his T- shirt. He laid them carefully on the tea table. The five thugs and others surrounded him to see. There was a small triangular sculpture that looked like a piece of a bigger sculpture. A knight holding a sword was sculpted on it. An arc on one of the angles of the triangle showed some lines indicating an incomplete sculpture. The other item was a sturdy metal key about six inches in length. This was probably the key to the treasure.

Before all of them could discuss, the voice spoke through Shiv's gadget, "Good job Shiv! I'd like you all to rest and be up for the five-a.m. flight to Thiruchirappalli via Mumbai."

Shiv looked up in surprise only to realize that the goons had already clicked pictures and sent them to the kidnapper.

"What! We are leaving tomorrow?" asked Saloni.

"It seems so. We don't have a choice," replied Nysa pointing at the goons who were leering at them.

Shiv looked at his friends and said, "The clue was the inscription that belonged to one of the four dynasties. Perhaps, we should look out for such a clue in our next destination too."

All the others agreed.

The goons gave them food packets brought from some cheap Chinese stall in the village. However, all of them were too famished to fuss or complain. After dinner, Nysa went to the bedroom to retire. Saloni walked over to Arjun who was sitting in the veranda. Tony and Shiv rested in the living room with the goons.

"I am going to miss this veranda," Saloni said to Arjun. "I have spent a few memorable moments with you here."

He looked at her and smiled extending his hand to hold hers, "I'll give you many more to remember."

Arjun was resting with his back and head against the wall and his legs spread straight. Saloni sat on his thighs with the back of her head resting on his chest. She spread her legs along his. She held his hands and placed them around her belly. She could feel his warm breath on the back of her neck. She could hear his heartbeat.

"I feel so safe with you," she said letting out a breath of relief.

Within a few minutes, she was asleep. The kidnapper was anxious. He could see the GPS trackers of Arjun and Saloni merge into one. He called up one of his goons who came into the veranda to check. The goon violently shook Arjun, who awakened with a start.

"Boss says no hanky-panky on the mission."

Arjun carried Saloni to the living room and placed her comfortably on the sofa. He covered her with a bed sheet and settled to sleep on the other sofa.

The kidnapper checked himself into a cheap motel outside the village. He settled on the bed, hoping to have a good time. He had installed a hidden camera in Tony's bedroom. With Saloni asleep, he was hoping for some skin show from Nysa. He had seen Nysa before in his captivity. She had a beautiful sultry body.

Nysa decided to take a shower. She stripped herself completely and lay down on the bed to relax. The kidnapper was aroused. When she moved to her side, he could see her breasts crush each other. Her perfect legs spread on the bed were so inviting. The curves of her hips and her flat belly turned him on. His hands reached his groin. Just then, there was a knock on Nysa's door.

She asked, "Who's there?"

"It's me," replied Shiv. "Just checking if you need anything, a bandage change or something."

Nysa smiled, wrapped a towel around herself and opened the door.

"Wow!" exclaimed Shiv smiling awkwardly.

"Was just going for a shower. Care to join?" she asked pulling him in the room and locking the door.

She went back to lying on the bed. He lay down beside her and watched her for a while. He then opened the bandage on her shoulder and checked the wound. The wound was healing well. He stroked the wound and her shoulder. She snuggled closer to him. He could feel that she was breathing fast and her heart was pounding.

The kidnapper was restless by now. After the mission, I am going to kill the two guys, he thought.

He got impatient and spoke through Shiv's gadget, "Leave the girl alone and get off the bed. Her wound is fine. She doesn't need a bandage change."

Shiv was alarmed. He asked Nysa if he could use her bathroom. She nodded. He came out and secretly handed her a chit. It was a good thing that he was carrying the piece of paper and pen he had taken from the coffee shop. She went into the bathroom and read the paper, 'He is watching this room.' Nysa was distressed. She came out and carried her clothes to the bathroom. You will pay for this Shiv, swore the kidnapper. Nysa rushed out into the living room, distraught and tearful. Shiv rushed to comfort her.

"I wanted you to be the only one to see me like this," she said.

"But…," said Shiv looking at Nysa. She was too distraught. It wasn't the right time to mention Raj Mittal, he thought.

He hugged her. "It's okay. It's not a big deal."

She hugged him back and they settled in a corner of the living room. Tony looked around for a place to lie down. Finding none, he went to the bedroom, stripped and went to sleep. The kidnapper was fuming at the obnoxious sight.

All of them reached Thiruchirappalli airport by noon. The gadgets on their wrists were well hidden by the full sleeved shirts given to them by the kidnapper. They easily passed through the metal detectors. The kidnapper had temporarily switched off the GPS trackers of the devices. They looked like ordinary watches. Shiv kept observing all the passengers in the aircraft to identify the kidnapper.

If what the kidnapper said was true, he had to remain within a certain radius of our devices, thought Shiv. The only way to do so was to remain on the same plane. Shiv could not identify any familiar face during his numerous intentional trips to the aircraft's front and back washrooms.

In the meantime, the kidnapper enjoyed watching Shiv's vain attempts to identify him. At one such instant, he stood right next to Shiv without raising any suspicion. He entered the ladies' washroom and checked his disguise. Perfect! I look like a perfect lady, he thought to himself.

At the airport, two private cars were hired for them. Shiv, Tony and three of the goons seated themselves in one car, and the remaining took another. After a while, the kidnapper emerged from the airport. A car was waiting for him.

It took two hours for them to reach Brihadisvara temple. The entry to the temple was prohibited in the afternoon hours. All of them had their meal at a restaurant near the temple. Shiv had managed to convince the kidnapper to let them hire a guide to gain information about the temple. The kidnapper had denied his initial request of letting him use the internet.

The temple gates were opened at around 4 p.m. The goons waited outside and the rest of them visited the temple. The temple was beautiful and huge. All of them were awestruck by its architectural grandeur. The premises outside the temple had a well-maintained lawn and lustrous green trees. The guide accompanying the five of them began talking,

"Welcome to one of the grandest temples of India. This temple has completed one thousand years in 2010. It was built by the Chola king Rajarajeshwara in the 11th century. The boundary wall around the temple was built much later in the 16th century."

"So, the boundary wall is out from our area of interest," said Arjun.

The guide continued, "The temple was built to celebrate a huge military victory by the king. The main deity of the temple is *Nataraja*, the dancing Shiva. The temple also has a huge *Shivalinga* and a huge Nandi statue, both about twelve feet tall."

Shiv and his friends were listening while simultaneously looking out for a clue. The guide took them around the temple and said, "This was the first temple to be entirely built using granite stones, which is not naturally available within a hundred kilometre radius of this temple, indicating that it was brought from farther than that. No one is aware about the original source of the granite stones."

All of them clicked photographs of all the sculptures on the outer wall of the temple. The tower of the temple was very high and Shiv hoped that the clue was not hidden there. None of them could find an inscription similar to the one found in Kandariya Mahadev Temple.

Inside the temple, all of them listened to the history of the temple and clicked several pictures. Fortunately, photography was not prohibited. They touched each sculpture to check for lose stones, chests and hidden spaces, but found nothing. By the time they came out, it was dark and the temple was lit up. The guide pointed to the top-most light over the temple tower. It shone like a beautiful celestial body.

"This was the tallest temple in the 11th century. The temple was the central part of a huge city built around it during that era," added the guide.

Although all of them were mesmerized by the brilliant workmanship of Indian architecture, they had not achieved their goal of finding the clue.

Just when they were about to leave, the guide asked them, "Will you be visiting Gangaikonda Cholapuram Temple? It was built by King Rajarajeshwara's son King Rajendra I. Many endowments from this temple were shifted to that temple after it was declared as the capital of Chola dynasty. Both temples are beautifully built, probably by the same artisans and architects. It is a must see."

All of them thanked the guide and moved to the car.

"Did you find anything?" asked the kidnapper through Shiv's gadget.

"Nothing," replied Shiv. "We may have to visit the Gangaikonda Cholapuram Temple tomorrow."

"Why?"

"Because our clue could have been moved there."

"What if you find nothing there?"

"Then, we may have to return to this temple."

The kidnapper was angry. This meant that the wait for his treasure would be longer.

"I think it's a good decision," affirmed Nysa looking at Shiv.

"Yes, I would move all my treasures along if I was moving to a new city. That would be most natural," added Arjun.

"Also, the treaty would have been signed during the father-son period. Hence, the chances of loss of information to the immediate next generation are minimal," said Saloni.

The road travel time from Brihadisvara Temple in Thanjavur to Gangaikonda Cholapuram Temple in Ariyalur was about an hour. Everyone halted for breakfast at an Udipi restaurant and reached the temple at about 10 a.m.

The courtyard of this temple was clean and beautifully maintained. A number of statues, some of them broken, were displayed on the premises. All of them went to see the statues. A board near the statues read:

The great city of Gangaikondacholapuram met with a catastrophe in the 12th century. Everything, except the temple, was destroyed. These statues were recovered by a team of archaeologists in the 20th century.

"These are not of our interest then," said Tony.

All of them formed two teams and walked around to check the outer premises of the temple. The number of sculptures here was fewer than in the previous temples. They touched the walls to check for possible storage spaces, but found none.

They entered the inner sanctum of the temple. All of them prayed to seek blessings from the Shivalinga. They moved around to scrutinize the walls judiciously. This temple was smaller and better illuminated than the previous two temples.

No sign of any circular inscription of any of the dynasties was discovered. They kept looking around until Tony saw something unusual. He pointed out to a sculpture on the wall six feet above the floor.

"This sculpture shows many snakes, which could be perfectly fine given the fact that this is a Shiva temple," said Nysa.

"Right, except that usually sculptures depict only one snake or show a snake with a Shivalinga or with a Shiva statue in Shiva temples. A group of snakes is unusual. Also, Mr Kapoor had mentioned that a group of snakes were protectors of the treasure. This could be considered a worthy clue," said Tony.

"He's got a point there," said Arjun.

"Just check instead of discussing," said Saloni getting impatient and irritable.

Shiv extended his hand to feel the sculpture. He could feel a small gap below the sculpture, probably made to pull out the chest. Shiv nodded and signalled everyone to take positions. Nysa, Tony and Saloni guarded the entrances.

Shiv removed the small bottle of oil from his pocket and poured it around the crevices. He struggled slightly and pulled out the stone. However, due to the height, he could not peep into the contents or reach into the chest. He climbed over Arjun's back and quickly extracted the contents and closed the chest.

All of them gathered in the temple courtyard and sat down in the lawn. The breeze was warm. Shiv looked all around and then showed them what he had retrieved. The contents included another key and a triangular piece of sculpture similar to the one retrieved from Kandariya Mahadev Temple. The only difference was in the design inside the arc at the angle of the triangular piece.

"Any luck?" came the voice through Arjun's gadget.

"Mission accomplished," replied Arjun.

"Good, I have a little surprise for Shiv," said the voice.

All of them hurried towards the car. The goons were waiting for them. One of the goons handed Shiv his phone with a video waiting to be played. Shiv clicked the play button. The video showed Mr Sanyal reclined on a bed.

He said, "Shiv, I know you are in trouble. I love you, son. I miss you and Arjun. Take care."

The video moved on to show Mr Ballad bound to a chair.

He said, "Saloni, sweetheart, I love you. Don't give whatever he wants. He is evil."

Just then, somebody punched him and taped his mouth. Saloni began weeping on seeing the video.

"Just wanted to show that Sanyal has recovered and Ballad is alive. I hope this is a good enough motivation to finish the task quickly," said the kidnapper. "Back to the hotel," he commanded.

All of them got into the car. The goons carefully collected the clues and kept them in a briefcase that contained clues from the previous temple. They stopped for a meal at an expensive place. The kidnapper's way of expressing happiness, they thought. The girls were anxious about entering their room. They were not sure which of the rooms would have cameras. What if he had installed cameras in both rooms? Shiv went to the reception and requested for a change of room. Only one room was available. Shiv asked the girls to shift to that room.

The kidnapper sat watching an empty room that night. He was going to avenge all this. He would make the girls pay dearly. For now, he decided to watch Nysa's beautiful body from the previous recording.

Shiv and Arjun went to the girls' room to check if they were comfortable. Tony was tired. He helped himself to some alcohol and went off to sleep. The room provided to the girls was a suite. Shiv and Nysa went into the inner room and Arjun and Saloni settled on the bed in the outer room.

"I am sorry about your dad," said Nysa sitting on the bed. "I wish they had released him instead of me."

"I love you both," said Shiv.

"Saloni narrated your dream to me. I have been bringing you bad luck over several lifetimes," continued Nysa, looking down.

"Do you believe my dream?" asked Shiv while sitting opposite her.

"Of course, I do. I always wondered about these scars on my ankle and back. Now I know," she replied.

"Nysa, I have waited so long to meet you. I wish we had met earlier," said Shiv gently placing his hands on her shoulders.

"Shiv, why do you care so much?"

"Because I... I...," hesitated Shiv.

"I what?" asked Nysa looking into Shiv's eyes.

Before Shiv could reply, the kidnapper's voice interrupted, "Time to go to bed, everyone. We have an early morning flight to Bengaluru."

"Damnit," cursed Shiv trying to control his passion.

In the outer room, Arjun comforted Saloni, "Your dad is going to be fine."

"I hope so," she said with sadness in her voice.

"Come here," said Arjun extending his arms.

Saloni was excited and rushed into his strong arms. He held her firmly wrapping his arms around her for a while. He then lifted her chin and kissed her.

In the airplane, Shiv and Arjun kept scanning the other passengers to identify the kidnapper. Meanwhile, the kidnapper was watching them closely. He was seated just two rows behind on the opposite side. He had a direct view of the girls. He was disguised as a bald old man with false teeth and round spectacles. He had even touched Nysa on his way into the flight on the pretext of taking support.

The kidnapper had booked private cars for them from Bengaluru airport to Kalleshwara Temple at Bagali, a distance that would be covered in two hours. They reached the temple in time of its open hours. The area around the temple was barren.

Kalleshwara Temple wasn't as grand as the other temples. It was built partly by two dynasties, the Rashtrakutas and the Western Chalukyas.

"We need to hire a guide to understand which part was built by which dynasty in order to identify our areas of interest," suggested Shiv.

The goons hired an English-speaking guide and all of them began their expedition. The temple was old and not very well maintained. It was constructed using soapstone and was falling apart at several places. A huge Nandi statue sat at the entrance. The outer hall was open and had fifty decorated pillars supporting an intricately carved ceiling. Shiv directed Tony and Arjun to search the outer hall, whereas he went into the inner sanctum with Nysa and Saloni.

A statue of Lord Shiva adorned the womb of the temple, with several sculptures decorating the inner walls. Shiv asked Nysa and Saloni to carefully inspect the inner sanctum because they had found clues in the womb of the other two temples. However, the walls of the womb of this temple were hollow at several places with pieces of sculptures missing or lying on the floor. The guide informed them that the womb was built by the Rashtrakuta dynasty. Shiv was relieved and decided to inspect the other shrines that were built in the Western Chalukya period.

Shiv, Saloni and Nysa returned to the outer hall. They were surprised by the scene in the outer hall.

"Looks like you two have recruited a whole bunch to help you out," said Shiv looking behind Arjun and Tony.

Arjun and Tony turned around and noticed that the tourists were imitating their act of palpating, tapping and putting their ears to the pillars. Some of them even claimed to have heard music, while others felt that some sculptures were inscribed in braille on the pillars.

"Humans did evolve from apes," commented Arjun chuckling.

Nysa and Saloni smiled at the view.

Tony informed, "No luck here."

"Let's move to the other shrines," said Shiv.

The other shrines too were falling apart at places. The guide informed that parts of the shrines had been restored at various stages in the past few centuries. The team inspected the remains of the shrine and found nothing of interest. They came back to the outer hall, dejected.

"What now?" asked Saloni throwing up her hands in despair.

"Who would know the history of the temple?" questioned Nysa.

"The temple caretaker," Tony replied promptly.

Arjun asked the guide about the temple caretaker. The guide directed them to the temple donation office. The caretaker was a middle-aged man. He spoke only Kannada. Shiv sought the guide's help for translation. The caretaker informed them that his father had been looking after the temple before the job was passed on to him. His ancestors had been doing the job from the time the temple was built. Shiv showed the caretaker a picture of the sculpture sent by the kidnapper. The caretaker knew nothing about it.

Arjun asked if they could meet his father. The caretaker was hesitant and asked them the reason for the meeting. Shiv explained he and his friends were researchers who were studying ancient Indian monuments. They intended to write a book about their research.

The caretaker was convinced and took them to meet his father in the quarters just outside the temple courtyard. The old caretaker was bedridden. The guide explained everything to the old man. Shiv showed him the picture of the sculpture. The old man strained to see, but his old eyes lit up after he recognized the picture. He looked at Shiv and folded his hands. Shiv held his hands and bowed to him. The old caretaker said that he was thankful that he was being relieved of the duty trusted upon him by his ancestors. He was going to pass on the treasure box to his son on his death bed to be preserved for someone who would come enquiring some day – a lore passed on by his ancestors. That had always been the tradition in his family. He requested everybody else to wait outside his house.

Shiv helped the old man sit up. He moved slowly and pointed at an old rusted iron chest below his bed. Shiv pulled out the chest. The old man handed him the key to the chest. Inside the chest were some old coins, jewellery and a rectangular cardboard box. The old man pointed at the box. Shiv brought out and kept the heavy box on the bed. The old man eagerly opened the box. It contained a drawer made of stone. Inside the drawer were familiar clue articles that Shiv was looking for. The old man picked up the key and the triangular piece of sculpture and handed them over to Shiv. He took the articles and took the old man's blessings. He glanced at the stone drawer and noted that it had a sculpture of date palm trees of Khajuraho, which would have been unusual in this temple. He spoke to the old man for a while and then took his leave. The old man had a look of relief and satisfaction on his face.

Shiv came out and signalled everyone to follow. They went to the car.

"Looks like you have found the third clue," said the voice through Shiv's gadget.

"Yes, but I will hand it over only after you keep your promise of releasing Mr Ballad and my dad," replied Shiv.

The kidnapper chuckled, "I told you I am a man of my words."

"I need proof."

"Very well, you have to wait for some time, but hand over the clues to my men. You don't really have a choice."

Shiv handed them the key and the piece of sculpture. They proceeded to a four-star hotel in the vicinity. In the evening, the goons showed Shiv and Saloni a video of Mr Ballad and Mr Sanyal in their respective homes. Saloni demanded to speak to her dad. The kidnapper allowed his men to dial the home numbers of Sanyal and Ballad. Shiv and Saloni spoke to their respective dads and were convinced that they had been released. The kidnapper had issued warnings to both the families against approaching the police.

The kidnapper had booked one double room for all five of them.

"My man will hand over the sculpture pieces to you to identify our place of interest," said the kidnapper through Tony's gadget.

The goons handed them the three triangular pieces of sculpture. Shiv took the pieces and assembled them together. After a few adjustments, they were able to view the complete picture of the puzzle.

The three triangular pieces when joined together formed one big triangle. The central part of the triangle had a circle formed by the arcs at the angle of each triangular piece. It showed date palm trees lining a road and a woman with folded hands at the end of the road. The Khajuraho picture was in the central circle and three warriors with swords were depicted in the rest of the part of each piece. Only Shiv knew that the sculpture belonged to Khajuraho.

"This was the western gate of Khajuraho," said Shiv.

"This statue no longer stands there," he added.

"I have never read or heard about this statue in any of the books. How do you know about it?" asked Tony.

Shiv looked at them and said, 'You know how I know about it."

"From this, it seems like the treaty was signed only between three dynasties," concluded Nysa.

"Meaning that the treasure is in Khajuraho," added Saloni.

"But where in Khajuraho?" asked Arjun.

"On the bank of a river," replied Tony pointing to the two wavy lines in the picture of the original sculpture.

"Do you recall seeing such a temple in Khajuraho?" Shiv asked Tony while pointing at the temple in the fourth part of the picture.

Tony shook his head sideways.

"Ok, this means we have to pack our bags and go back to Khajuraho," interrupted the voice through Saloni's gadget. "Let's celebrate tonight while I make arrangements for the travel."

The kidnapper sent a few clothes for them. Nysa wore a beige off-shoulder knee length frock and Saloni wore a blood red short frock. The kidnapper saw them through the camera and was pleased. Blood and skin were his favourite colours.

He wore a wig, black-rimmed rectangular glasses and a false nose. He dressed himself in a light-yellow polo T-shirt and a pair of black jeans. He was pleased to see himself. He looked at least a decade younger than his actual age. Perhaps, the girls would notice him, he hoped.

Shiv and Arjun were awestruck on seeing Nysa and Saloni. They looked ravishing. Shiv was worried about the intentions of the kidnapper. On several occasions, Shiv and Arjun had tried to find the identity of the kidnapper. However, the trials were subtle, bearing in mind that he always had eyes and ears on them.

Shiv, Arjun and Tony were given casual shirts and jeans. However, even the casual short-sleeved shirts looked great on Shiv and Arjun due to their fit physique. They went down to the pub. It was crowded. All five of them settled around a table. They noticed that the goons were seated on a nearby table and were watching them. The kidnapper sat in a dark corner and admired the girls.

Tony ordered tequila shots for everyone. He ordered a few extra rounds for himself.

"I am glad we are going back home tomorrow. I am homesick," said Tony.

Shiv comforted him and raised a toast, "To Khajuraho."

All the others cheered. After a while, a young pretty girl approached Shiv and requested a dance. Shiv being a gentleman was unable to refuse.

He looked at Nysa and asked, "Shall I?"

Nysa looked upset, but she smiled and said, "Go ahead."

Shiv was confused, but before he could respond, the girl pulled him away. Nysa gulped the extra tequila shots that Tony had ordered.

Tony warned her, "Easy Nysa madam."

She suddenly got up and approached the kidnapper and requested him to dance. The kidnapper was thrilled. He obliged. Nysa was too drunk to look at the kidnapper carefully.

While dancing, Shiv looked at the table and noticed that Nysa was missing. He looked around the room and saw her dancing with a stranger. He noticed the hands of the stranger moving on her back and waist. She was dancing too close to the stranger. Shiv excused himself from the girl and tapped on the shoulder of the stranger. The stranger moved away without turning to face Shiv. He feared being recognized. He slipped back to his dark corner.

Shiv supported Nysa and asked her angrily, "What do you think you are doing?"

"Sweet vengeance. I am done being good and decent," she said looking at him with bloodshot eyes.

"Vengeance for what?"

She stamped Shiv's foot and said, "For making me jealous."

"Ouch," said Shiv staggering on his feet. He placed his hands on her cheeks, and she did the same. She was tipsy with all the alcohol in her system. He kissed her lightly on her lips, and she kissed him back passionately. He smiled and placed her hand on the left side of his chest. To his surprise, she placed his hand on her chest. Shiv was stunned. He could feel the loud pounding of her heart.

He moved his hand away and whispered, "Nysa, is this your first time?"

Nysa pushed him away, "Why do you keep asking me that? Does it matter so much to you?"

"No, it's not that. Your heart is beating so fast, like it could explode any minute. If it is your first time, I want to be gentle and slow," said Shiv, pulling her back towards him.

"I don't want you to be gentle. Come on to me with all that you have. Understand?" said Nysa staggering.

Shiv supported her and said, "Time for you to go to bed. You can hardly stand."

"No, I want to dance," said Nysa resisting his attempts to hold her.

He disregarded her wish, carried her in his arms and moved towards the elevator. She was too drunk to protest. The kidnapper was watching all the drama. He went up to his room to keep a watch on Shiv. In the room, Shiv gently laid Nysa on the bed.

She held on to him, "I am not letting you go."

"You are too drunk to comprehend what you are asking for."

She held his shirt and strongly pulled him closer, "Not as much as you think."

He tried to pull himself back but she didn't let him go, not this time. The tug of war resulted in tearing of Shiv's shirt, exposing his chest. He looked down at her. She was breathing fast. Her pretty legs were restless. Her tensed neck with the beauty spot and her smooth shoulders looked inviting. Her grip on the torn ends of his shirt was firm.

"What the hell! I give up," said Shiv and embraced her.

He pressed her against his body.

"Oh Shiv," she sighed and clawed into his back.

He buried his face into her chest.

"Hey Shiv, hold your horses. Taking advantage of a drunken girl? Too bad!" shrieked the kidnapper's voice.

"He's watching us," whispered Shiv into Nysa's ears. "You have to let me go."

Nysa did not loosen her grip, "I don't care."

Shiv pulled himself away from her and said, "I do."

He covered her with a bed sheet and sat on the bed cursing the kidnapper and wringing his hands. He then went into the living room and punched into the wall with frustration.

Meanwhile, in the pub, Tony continued his drunken spree. One of Saloni's favourite Hollywood numbers was playing. Tony had consumed so much alcohol that he wanted to puke. Arjun helped him to the washroom. Saloni was unable to control and began dancing on the dance floor. The goons noticed that Saloni was alone. The two goons who had earlier tried to grope Saloni went to the dance floor and began dancing uncomfortably close to her. She resisted, but they did not let her go. They sandwiched her between them.

Arjun came back from the washroom and saw Saloni's plight. He briskly moved to the dance floor and pushed away both the goons. Saloni hugged him and began crying. He took her to the table and made her sit down comfortably.

He went back to the dance floor and whispered something to the goons. The goons and Arjun went out of the pub. After a while, only Arjun returned. Saloni noticed a little blood trickling from one corner of his lips. She noticed a few bruises on his knuckles as well. Arjun, Saloni and Tony went back to the room.

Saloni went straight into the bedroom. Tony collapsed on the sofa in the living room. Arjun looked at Shiv. He was staring outside the window. He turned to see Arjun.

Arjun noticed his torn shirt, "Really? Now?" he taunted. "You couldn't even wait to unbutton it, huh? Just tore it off?"

Shiv walked out of the room. Arjun followed.

"Tell Saloni the room is under watch," said Shiv.

"I already did that," replied Arjun.

"What happened?" asked Arjun holding his torn shirt.

Shiv looked at the blood on Arjun's face and the bruises on his fist and asked, "What happened to you?"

He began wiping the blood off the corner of Arjun's lips when a young man walked in the corridor and asked, "Lovers' tiff, huh?"

Shiv looked at Arjun and chuckled, "Really? Is that how we look?"

Arjun too chuckled and replied, "I am afraid so."

The kidnapper was watching the girls in their rooms. He had the good luck of being able to touch Nysa today. He was aroused on remembering the feeling when his hands were moving up and down her waist and back. Her curves were so perfect and her skin so smooth. He had managed to peep and see her cleavage while dancing. He touched his chest on the places she had rested her hands. Her smile was so intoxicating. She looked so sensual when she moved her hand into her lustrous hair.

He looked at Saloni. She was asleep. She looked pure and innocent like an angel. He alternately licked the chocolate and vanilla cones that he had brought with him to his room. He had to find a quick replacement for the two goons that Arjun had beaten down. They deserved what they got, he thought.

Tony felt blessed to have reached his home in Khajuraho. He had missed his village and his men. Everyone rested for a couple of hours in the afternoon.

In the evening, the kidnapper spoke through Shiv's gadget, "We have to find the fourth temple to find the treasure. All of you get to work."

"We are going to need the internet," said Saloni.

"Okay. My men will supervise your access," said the kidnapper.

Saloni searched for rivers flowing through Khajuraho.

"You don't need internet for this," said Tony. "The only river closest to Khajuraho is Ken. The banks of the river are rocky at some places. The river flows into deep gorges and through dense forest at other places. The forest has wild animals and is infested with snakes and crocodiles."

He took a break and shuddered after mentioning snakes. He had visible goose bumps.

"A couple of lodges are located at the open areas of the river banks. The river is navigable only up to a certain point. It is dangerous to follow the river through the forest and it may take several days, that is, if we survive," he added.

Everyone was listening carefully.

"What if we can manage an aerial view?" asked Arjun.

"You mean a satellite view?" asked Saloni.

"No, I mean if we can hire a helicopter to recce the area," replied Arjun.

"Is that possible?" asked Nysa.

Everyone looked at Tony.

"I can try," he replied.

"Very well then, my men will accompany Tony and try to hire a helicopter," said the voice through Tony's gadget.

"There's a helipad twenty kilometres from here. I'll explode much earlier with my wrist gadget set at five kilometres," said Tony expressing his concern to the kidnapper.

"Don't worry, I'll feed new settings for today," replied the voice.

Tony left in the evening with two of the goons. He returned at around 9 p.m. after making arrangements for the coming morning.

"We have hired two helicopters with a capacity of seven passengers plus a pilot in each. We start at eight tomorrow."

The kidnapper would be in one of the two helicopters, thought Shiv. Tomorrow is a big day. Finally, we will be free.

You will never be able to catch me, thought the kidnapper. Tomorrow, I shall be one of the richest men in the country. Tomorrow will be your last day alive. Tomorrow, the girls will be mine forever.

Shiv and his friends played cards for some time to take their minds off the coming day. All of them slept in the living room. The goons, including the two new members, kept a watch over them in turns in the veranda. The kidnapper settled in his motel room outside the village.

Next morning, everyone was up early. Tony had requested the kidnapper for gumboots, leather jackets and shades for everyone. The kidnapper had obliged. They left for the helipad in two cars. The kidnapper followed at a distance. The paperwork was done by Tony and their rides were ready for take-off. They were to fly over the route of Ken River. All five of them, along with two armed goons, settled in one helicopter and the rest in another.

Shiv was disappointed for not being able to get a glimpse of the kidnapper. Both the rides were in visible distance of each other. They looked down to view the river. Nysa was dizzy and closed her eyes. Saloni was thrilled and felt like she was acting in a Hollywood movie.

Shiv, Arjun and Tony carefully looked down at the river and its banks. There were no temples in the open areas of the river banks. The rocky areas were too deep and rough for human exploration. Building a temple and hiding a treasure was impossible in this area. That left only the forest to be explored.

Shiv requested the pilot to go slow over the forest area. They did not notice anything worthy in their first round. Arjun requested the pilot to lower the flying height. At the low height, the breeze generated from the movement of the helicopter separated the thick foliage and provided a better view.

Suddenly, Saloni shouted looking through her binoculars, "I saw something in that foliage," she said pointing towards a thicket of trees.

All of them looked in that direction. The helicopter flew over the area again. A white structure was visible to them. They could not make out the details, but it seemed to be man-made.

The pilot communicated with the pilot of the other helicopter. The nearest landing site from the thicket was at the bank of the river. From there, the team would have to walk south towards the forest for at least one kilometre.

Both the helicopters landed. Shiv was handed a compass for directions and distance. He and Arjun looked behind to identify the kidnapper. There was an extra person in the group behind. Three of the goons and the kidnapper were wearing netted masks. It was impossible to tell which one of them was the kidnapper. Damn, thought Shiv.

They kept moving. The forest was getting thicker. All of them were worried about Tony. He was prone to attacks by cobras. Tony was careful and watchful. They heard some sounds of wild animals near the river bank, but kept walking. After about thirty minutes, they reached their target place. The ground around the place was covered with layers of shed snake skin interspersed with *bael* fruits and leaves. All of them were breathing fast in fear of being bitten by snakes.

The structure they saw left them astounded. A six feet tall idol of Lord Shiva made of black marble was installed at the center of a raised white marble circular platform. A Nandi idol, about three feet tall and made of white stone was installed in front of the Shiva idol. The circular platform had a height of two feet and a diameter of eight feet.

Around the structure was a clear area of about three feet. The perimeter of the clear area was lined by dense foliage of huge *bael* trees.

"Not all plans meet completion," murmured Shiv.

Everyone looked at him.

He said, "These were the words of Devi ji. Looks like this is our place, the only temple in Khajuraho in which the inner sanctum was built before the outer sanctum. The temple construction was never completed."

The kidnapper stepped forward and climbed the platform.

"Good job everyone. Get the treasure keys," he said holding a gun and beckoning one of his men.

Shiv and Arjun were unable to identify him through the mask. Arjun noticed a bulge in his upper pocket, the remote control, he thought. Saloni too noticed it. Arjun calculated the distance between himself and the kidnapper. It was around four feet, which included climbing the platform. This would require about two to three steps and the same number of seconds. The reflex action for the goons behind him to fire would be five seconds. He had an extra time of two seconds. What if the kidnapper shot him from the front? He had to wait until the kidnapper's finger was off the trigger. Arjun was intently watching every move of the kidnapper for the right opportunity.

One of the goons stepped forward to hand over the keys to the kidnapper. All the other goons were distracted. Arjun knew this was his chance. He lunged forward and snatched the gun of the goon who had climbed the platform to hand over the keys, and pointed it at the back of the kidnapper's head. The kidnapper raised his hands in the air. Arjun asked the other goons to put down their guns. Shiv, Tony, Saloni and Nysa picked up their guns. Arjun took away the kidnapper's gun. He removed the remote from the kidnapper's pocket and handed it to Saloni.

The remote had a red button, a green button and several numbered buttons. Saloni was perplexed.

She muttered, "Too many buttons." She asked Shiv and Tony, "Red or green?"

Shiv said red and Tony said green. Saloni asked Nysa. Nysa shrugged her shoulders. Saloni couldn't make up her mind. Red means stop, but it is also a colour used to indicate danger. Besides, the lights flickering on their gadget was green. She asked the kidnapper, who chuckled and refused to answer. She held her hand that had the gadget close to his face and was about to press the red button.

She said, "If we die, you die with us."

The kidnapper screamed, "No! It will explode in my face. Press the green button."

Saloni pressed the green button. Everyone's gadget made a clicking sound and unclasped. The green light went off. All of them removed the gadgets and destroyed them by stamping on them.

Nysa looked at her gadget and said, "Shiv, mine is still on."

Before Shiv could respond, the kidnapper held out another remote from his back pocket and kept his finger on the red button.

He said to Shiv, "She was put on a gadget with a different remote control. You forgot that she was already wearing the gadget when I sent her to Tony's house. All of you drop the guns or I will press the button."

Shiv was alarmed. He dropped the gun and asked the others to do the same. The goons and the kidnapper picked up their guns and pointed at each of them. The kidnapper walked to Arjun and punched and kicked him in his stomach. Arjun fell on the ground. Shiv and Tony were about to help him get up when the kidnapper kicked Tony on his back.

He punched Shiv and said, "I tried to be nice to you and see what your friends did. Did you really think that I brought Nysa here as a surprise gift for you? She was brought here to be of use when necessary. But like you, I too have fallen in love with her. In fact, I have fallen in love with both the girls," he said laughing aloud.

He put his arm around Nysa's waist and took her to the platform. "That day you danced with me when you were drunk. I can never forget how your body felt," he said flaring his nostrils, moving his hands over Nysa's back and kissing her neck. Nysa winced.

Shiv was getting restless. Arjun held Shiv's arm to hold him back.

"But love can wait. Work comes first," the kidnapper said, lightly touching Nysa's lips. "Everyone, search the place and find the keyholes for these keys," he said to his men.

Everyone scattered around the platform. No such points were visible. They looked at the Nandi statue. Nothing again. Only the Shiva idol remained to be inspected.

The kidnapper pointed his gun at Nysa and said to Shiv, "Tell me how to use these keys or she dies."

Shiv asked the kidnapper to allow him on the platform to inspect the idol. As soon as Shiv stepped on the platform, every one heard some sudden hissing and rustling sounds. There was chaos. Everyone looked around for snakes, but could see none. He moved closer to the idol, circled around it and prayed. He inspected the trident and the *damaru*. He looked at the Lord's face. The sculpture was divine.

A little breeze flowed, moving the tree branches around the platform and letting some sunshine fall on Lord Shiva's face. In the sunshine, Shiv saw the three keyholes, skillfully camouflaged at the intersection points of the three horizontal ashen lines on Lord Shiva's forehead with the vertical line depicting his closed third eye.

"These are the keyholes," said Shiv pointing at the idol's forehead.

The kidnapper released Nysa and stepped forward to check.

"Smart boy! I was right in picking you to find the treasure," he said.

He asked Shiv to step down from the platform. Shiv glanced at Nysa. She was distraught and was chewing the inside of her right cheek. His heart went out to her. He wanted to rush and comfort her, but instead, he stepped down.

The kidnapper asked his men to insert the keys. One of his goons inserted all the three keys. He turned the first key. A sound of some moving metal was heard below the platform. The hissing sound became more intense. The turning of the second key had the same effect. The goon tried to turn the third key, but it was stuck.

Shiv remembered that he had given the wrong key to the kidnapper's men in a bid to have an upper hand. He had given them the key of the old man's chest. Shiv slipped the third key in his hands from his jacket.

He spoke, "It requires a special technique shown to me by the old man. But I will show it only if you release Nysa."

The kidnapper chuckled, "You really think you are in a position to bargain with me? Just step up here and turn the key or all your other friends die."

Shiv removed the third key from the keyhole and acted as if he was inspecting it. He swapped the key with the one he had. He reinserted the original third key and turned it around. Almost immediately, a small trapdoor between Nandi's and Lord Shiva's statue fell open. It created a rectangular gap of about three feet by four feet in the platform.

The kidnapper stepped forward to peep. He could see some glittering precious stones and gold. His eyes were gleaming with greed. Taking advantage of the distraction, Shiv moved to comfort Nysa. The hissing sound was very loud by now, but no snakes were visible in the vicinity. The kidnapper asked one of his men to hand him a torch. In the torchlight, he could see that the floor was five feet below. There was a metal ladder hanging from the edge of the trapdoor. Piles of gold jewellery, gold coins, silver jewellery, silver coins, diamonds, rubies, pearls and sapphires were neatly arranged. He peeped inside and saw that the place was wider inside than the platform above.

"Okay folks, it's time to say goodbye," he said.

He looked at his men and directed, "Two of you kill the men and watch the girls. Three of you follow me with the bags. We may have to make several rounds to the helicopter."

"Won't you tell us who you are before killing us?" asked Shiv unable to hide his anger and helplessness.

He chuckled, "Sir, what would you like to have for dinner? Your suit is ready. You don't look too well today. Is there anything I can do? Your guests are comfortably seated in the living room."

Shiv frowned, "Bijlani?"

The kidnapper removed his mask and the voice modifier strapped to his mouth and said, "Yes sir, your loyal and personal caretaker."

"Why?" asked Shiv stunned.

"That's a rather silly question. Aren't my intentions obvious? I have sold off every valuable artwork from Sanyal House and replaced them with fakes. I learnt about this artwork leading to a treasure, but couldn't find it in Sanyal House. I swapped Mr Sanyal's hypertension medicines. I threatened him to tell me about this sculpture, but the man was stubborn. I gave him a dose of medicines that increased his blood pressure and he suffered a stroke. I left him to die. But your friend Arjun spoilt my plan. He informed Ballad and called for an ambulance. I played along. I had already hired Tony to kill you. But you had a lucky escape. Then I learnt of this girl who jumped in to save your life. Silly girl! I decided to have some fun. I changed my plan. I kidnapped her, Sanyal and Ballad to get you to find the sculpture for me. You couldn't find the sculpture, but you offered a better deal. I am still curious about where the sculpture is?"

"Why did you order my kidnapping?" asked Arjun.

"Me? What would I get by kidnapping a poor orphan? But I was glad you were kidnapped because you were always a threat to my plan," said the kidnapper.

Arjun was wondering about who had kidnapped him.

"All of you, happy now? You can all die peacefully now. I'll take the girls with me and enjoy them until they last."

Shiv was fuming with anger. As a reflex action, he pushed Bijlani into the trap door. Tony and Arjun acted quickly and thrashed the goons. Saloni snatched away the guns. In a few minutes, the goons were lying unconscious on the floor. All the goons and the guns were overpowered and Bijlani was in the treasure trench.

Shiv prepared to enter the trench through the trapdoor when Nysa stopped him, "No, wait! This can be dangerous. I don't like the sounds that are coming from inside. You all go away. It's not safe here. I'll stay here."

Shiv fixed his gaze on her and said, "You know I won't do that."

He climbed down the ladder. Inside, Bijlani was recovering from his fall. Shiv looked around. Numerous cobras were sitting with their hoods spread wide. They were guarding the treasure bags.

Bijlani pointed a gun at Shiv, "Looks like I won't come out of this, but I won't let you win."

Just when he was about to fire, Arjun fired from above the platform. Bijlani was hit on his right shoulder. He collapsed. The gun shot sound caused a commotion among the reptiles. Some of them began crawling out of the trap door. Shiv moved towards Bijlani to snatch the remote. Bijlani stood up quickly and began stamping on the remote. The remote was completely damaged. Bijlani picked up the broken remote and threw it on a group of cobras in a corner. A cobra from the group flung back at Bijlani and bit him on his forehead. Bijlani fell to the ground.

Everything around him was becoming hazy. He shook his head violently, still hazy. No…this is not the end. This can't be it. I can't die. I'll nap for a while and be back for my treasure, he thought. He looked around greedily at the gold and diamond bags. He could see Shiv leaning over him. I am going to get you…someday. He felt some fluid flowing out of his nose and mouth. He touched and saw blood and froth. He felt sharp pain in his chest, like someone was sitting on it and pushing out the last remaining breath out of his mouth. His breathing became very labourious. Within seconds, he was dead.

Shiv looked around for the remote. It was nowhere in sight. The cobras had probably moved it into one of their burrows. Shiv climbed out through the trap door. Nysa was staring in shock at her wrist device. A timer was ticking on the display. A timer set for 180 minutes! The green light was flickering.

"It's going to explode in 180 minutes!" shrieked Nysa looking helplessly at Shiv.

Shiv rushed towards her. At the same time, Tony screamed. A cobra had bit him through his thick pants. He was lying on the ground.

"Tony!" screamed Shiv and all of them rushed towards him.

He was pointing towards his jacket pocket. Saloni quickly reached for his pocket. It had a syringe and a needle labelled 'anti-snake venom'. Saloni quickly injected it into Tony's arm. Arjun looked at her in surprise. Tony began recovering. The timer on Nysa's hand displayed 170 minutes. She sat down in distress.

Shiv sat beside her, relieved her inner cheek from her bite and hugged her, "We will find a way to get rid of this."

"That's not possible. Any tampering will make it explode immediately. Shiv, I am trapped in the same situation again. You have to go away this time. You have to save yourself. Please, for my sake. We have to break this cycle."

"You think going away from you will save me?" asked Shiv. "Let's fly out of this place and find a solution. I'll go and search for the remote inside."

"You are not entering there again," ordered Nysa.

They all sat thinking for a while. Arjun entered the trench to locate the remote. It wasn't visible anywhere. There were too many snakes. The remote could be in any of the snake burrows. Even if the damaged remote was found, getting high tech help in two hours in a city like Khajuraho is impossible, he thought.

"Okay guys, it's time you all move back to the helicopter. I'll stay back with her," said Shiv standing up.

"No, we are not leaving you alone, not this time," said Arjun firmly.

Tony tried to get up and said, "Yes Shiv sir, we are not leaving."

"Let's first move away from this hell hole. It's creepy and infested with snakes," said Saloni.

Arjun and Saloni checked on the goons. They were still unconscious. Arjun and Saloni took the wallets and phones of the goons and threw their guns in the trench. They moved away and began walking through the thicket of trees.

After reaching a clear area, Shiv told Arjun, "Arjun, buddy, you have to go back and take care of dad and Saloni. You two have a good life."

Arjun did not budge from his decision. Shiv had to do a lot of talking to convince Arjun to back off. Arjun hugged him tightly. Saloni and Tony joined Arjun.

"It's okay. We are going to be fine. Tell dad that I love him. I am sorry I couldn't be there for him," said Shiv with tears welling up his eyes.

"You don't have to do this," said Nysa.

"You know I have to," replied Shiv.

"Why?" asked Nysa with tears in her eyes.

Shiv went to her, looked into her eyes and said, "Because I love you. I love you so much that I don't mind dying just to be with you."

"Aww," said Saloni looking at the two with tears in her eyes.

All of them hugged and cried for a while and parted ways. Nysa and Shiv moved towards the forest.

Shiv and Nysa walked hand in hand for a while, taking time to recover and reconcile to the fact that they were going to die. Shiv then moved closer to Nysa, put his arms around her shoulders and smiled.

"Why are you smiling?" asked Nysa.

"This forest holds a special place in our lives. We first met here, we lived here as a couple, wandered here and spent a lot of time with each other. We spent our last day in our past lives in this forest and now here we are again, awaiting our death in this forest," replied Shiv.

"The only progress we have made is that we have killed the villain this time," continued Shiv.

"Yes, that's good progress. At this rate, we may get married in the next few lifetimes. Until then, we may have to continue with wall punching and water splashing," tittered Nysa with tearful eyes.

Nysa looked at him and said, "We plan so ahead in life believing that we are invincible, but life is so fragile and unpredictable. I wish I had done so many things differently. It feels strange that I won't be alive in a few hours from now."

"We," corrected Shiv.

"Huh?" she looked at him.

"We won't be alive," he repeated. "Promise me that you will meet me earlier in our next life. Waiting until the age of twenty-eight is killing."

"You want us to meet again?"

Shiv looked at her in surprise, "Don't you?"

"Not like this. I don't want to come as your death warrant in every life. I hate myself for this."

"No! Don't hate yourself. It's nobody's fault, just a fault in our stars," winked Shiv.

He put her scattered hair strands behind her ears, kissed her forehead and hugged her tightly.

"I have a confession to make," said Nysa.

"Go ahead, I am listening," replied Shiv.

"You always kept asking if it was my first time."

"Yes? What about it?"

"It was my first time. I lied."

"You mean you have never... what about Raj Mittal?"

"I do occasionally accompany Mr Raj Mittal to parties and events, but I mainly work for Raj Mittal, junior."

"So?"

"The full name is Rajshri Mittal. She is a woman and she is straight. Raj Mittal senior has a mistress named Nisha. So, I sometimes use the confusion to my advantage."

Shiv was shocked. "But why did you lie?"

"To drive you away," replied Nysa looking down.

"Why?" asked Shiv lifting her chin.

"I guess I didn't want to hurt myself by falling in love with you," replied Nysa biting her cheek from inside and creating a dimple outside.

Shiv hugged her tightly. They stood silently embracing each other for some time.

"You have made love to many women; how do they feel after the act?" she asked, embarrassed. "Just curious because I have never been there."

"Do you want to be there?" asked Shiv looking into her eyes.

"Now? Here? You don't want us to be married this time?"

He chuckled and said, "That was the 11th century, but I'll wait if you want that."

She blushed and said, "I was ready even back then. And I have made my intentions fairly clear ample number of times in this lifetime too, haven't I?"

He looked at the compass. They were just two metres away from crossing the five kilometre mark. He moved ahead and drew a line in the mud with a stick.

"Beyond this line lies our next life," he said looking at Nysa.

She looked at her timer. They had ninety minutes.

He came back to her. "I know you guys are around. Back off and give us some privacy. Move out of our audio and visual ranges," shouted Shiv.

Nysa looked at him questionably, "Some ritual to ward off evil spirits before the act?"

"No!" laughed Shiv. "It's for Arjun, Tony and Saloni. They are trailing us."

They heard some movement in the bushes behind them. Shiv took a deep breath to relax and forget the impending death. Nysa was breathing fast, but not due to fear of death. He kissed her passionately on her lips. She responded with equal passion. He removed their jackets and spread them on the ground. He unbuttoned her shirt. Every touch of his fingers ran a current through her body. He reached for her gumboots and pants. He undressed himself and looked at her.

"You are beautiful," he said.

She was embarrassed and looked down.

After a while, she gathered courage to look at him and said, "You are not so bad either."

He laughed. She was shaking.

He embraced to comfort her and whispered, "Are you sure?"

"Have never been surer," she replied.

He moved his hands and caressed her sultry body. She moaned and her muscles contracted involuntarily responding to his touches and kisses. He sensed her fast heartbeats and slowed down.

"Don't stop," she pleaded.

She felt his strong arms closing around her. She had never felt so thrilled yet secure.

Behind in the bushes, Saloni was weeping. She had known Shiv from her childhood. He was the most decent guy she had ever known. She had openly expressed her desire for him, but he had never misused his position. In fact, he had never laid a finger on her. Moreover, he had never made her feel embarrassed, cheap, or hurt while rejecting her.

Tony was standing and staring into the forest. He was smoking to get over his helplessness. Shiv had saved his life twice and there was no way of repaying the good man. Tony didn't like to bear the burden of unpaid good deeds. He was unable to watch the pain of a couple so much in love.

Arjun saw Tony smoking and began crying like a child. He remembered all the good times he had spent with Shiv. Shiv had been like a protective big brother. He was his emotional anchor after he lost his parents at a young age. They went to school and college together. They had their first beer together. They had discussed about their first crush and their first love experience. They had no secrets.

Unable to bear the pain, Arjun got up. He looked at the goon's mobile for a signal. There was none. If he could find some technical help over the phone, maybe they could unlock the device, he thought. He began climbing a tall tree to catch a signal. When he reached a good height, he moved his phone around to catch a signal. He looked around and saw Shiv and Nysa. He saw two nude bodies with one soul. They were so lost into each other that time had stopped for them. Tears began rolling down Arjun's eyes. He closed his eyes and looked the other way.

Shiv and Nysa were exploring each other. By now, they had become comfortable with each other's physical closeness. Nysa had lowered her shields and Shiv was taking her through an experience she had never had before. She felt him explode inside her. The first time was a little painful, but in the subsequent acts, the ecstasy overpowered the pain. He eased her through the act by constantly whispering 'I love you' in her ears. She had never felt so loved and wanted. They belonged to a different world with no time, space and fears.

She whispered 'Thank you' into Shiv's ears.

"The pleasure was all mine," he replied.

They lay there in each other's arms for a long time. Nysa looked at the timer, only five minutes were remaining. The feeling of impending doom rushed back. With great effort, she gathered herself.

Shiv looked at her and asked, "What happened?"

"Don't want anyone to find me nude after I die," she replied and began wearing her clothes.

Shiv too got up and put on his pants. Nysa was shaking with fear.

He pulled her towards him and said, "It's going to be alright. I'll take you through."

"Oh Shiv! Why do you love me so much? I want us to live," she started weeping.

Shiv held her hand that had the device and rested it on his shoulder. He hugged her tightly. Tears rolled down his eyes. She looked at the device, only twenty seconds were remaining.

She put her hands between Shiv and herself and gathered all her strength.

She looked into Shiv's eyes and said, "I shall always love you."

She pushed him away with all her strength. He fell down. He saw her running across the mud line.

"No Nysa," he shouted.

She crossed the line and turned around to see him for one last time. She wanted to hold his image in her soul forever. She tripped while turning. Shiv got up to help her. He leaped over the line to reach her. He lay down on her to protect her. He held her hand tightly. They heard a clicking sound and the device unclasped. Shiv looked at the device, it displayed 'Out of range.' Within seconds, Arjun, Tony and Saloni were embracing the couple.

Shiv looked at them with tears rolling down his eyes, "You fools!"

He looked at Arjun. He was crying like a baby. Shiv hugged him tightly and kissed him on his forehead.

Saloni moved closer to Nysa and asked, "You sure they are not gay?"

"I am sure about my man," replied Nysa.

"Hmm. I'll find out about Arjun soon enough," muttered Saloni.

"This means that the device had a range of five kilometres. If Nysa wouldn't have done what she did, you both would have been dead," said Saloni.

"Why did you do that, Nysa?" Shiv asked angrily.

"You wanted to die for me, I wanted you to live for me," replied Nysa.

"I didn't have the heart to let you die for me. Not again," she said hugging Shiv. Shiv hugged her back.

"Someone please tell me that there is a way out of this forest," said Shiv looking at everyone.

"Don't worry. In no time, the police and news channels will be combing the entire forest," replied Tony.

Arjun, Shiv and Nysa looked at Tony.

"It was Saloni madam's idea to ask my men to trail us. She even made me carry the snake bite anti-dote," replied Tony looking at Saloni with gratitude.

Arjun raised one of his eyebrows and tilted his head to show that he was impressed with Saloni.

"Bless you, Hollywood," he said.

He moved closer to Saloni and whispered, "Congratulations!"

"For what?" asked Saloni.

"For becoming the new boss of the don of Khajuraho," replied Arjun looking at Tony. Tony was standing with his hands folded and looking admirably at Saloni.

"No ... no ... no ... no," said Saloni and went about explaining something to Tony. They all had a hearty laugh.

It was their last night in Khajuraho. Arjun had gone out for some work.

When he returned to Tony's house, Tony was speaking over the phone to the director of Haffkine's institute, "What do you mean you can't manufacture a vaccine for one person? I am stalked by cobras and in immediate need of being vaccinated against cobra bite … Hmm … Okay … that's right … what research and trial? How many people are required? Okay. I'll get back to you soon."

He summoned his man and said, "Ask Natarajan to set up a website for people who are stalked by cobras. We need at least five hundred registrations to start research and trial for anti-cobra vaccine."

Arjun was waiting for Tony to finish his instructions.

Tony looked at Arjun and asked, "All fine?"

"Yup. It's just that I require this list of things ready in a few minutes," said Arjun handing over a sheet of paper to Tony.

Tony took the list, gave it to one of his men and ordered, "Now!"

Saloni was talking over the phone with Mr Ballad when Arjun approached her. "I am fine dad … no, I never went to Goa … I am sorry dad. I promise I'll never do it again … Yes, I was safe … No dad, not Shiv, it's Arjun … Yes, you heard it right, Arjun. Yes, I am sure … I'll explain when I come back tomorrow."

Arjun looked at her and asked, "All okay?" Saloni nodded.

She closed her eyes, took a deep breath and said, "You smell good."

"Thanks. Want to come for a really long drive with me?"

"Now?"

Arjun nodded.

"Okay," she replied.

"Okay then. Go up to the bedroom and you'll find something for you. I want you to dress for the occasion?"

Saloni raised her eyebrows in curiosity and asked, "What do you have in mind?"

"Do you trust me?"

"Yes, I do."

"Then go."

Arjun went back to Tony and asked, "Where are Shiv and Nysa?"

Tony pointed towards the veranda. They went to check on them. Shiv and Nysa were standing in the pose of 'eternal embrace'. Arjun looked down at Nysa's legs. Her right leg was away from Shiv, but after a while, she pulled her leg towards Shiv. A crescent moon was shining in the backdrop. Arjun and Tony stood with their arms around each other's shoulders and watched them for a while.

"God bless them," said Tony and moved in.

Arjun followed Tony and handed him a packet of food. "Just eat whenever you all are hungry. I'll get a little late."

He smiled, "Take your time."

Saloni dressed up and came down to the living room. She looked gorgeous. She was dressed in an off-shoulder little black dress. Her hair was loose and the subtle nude makeup worked wonders on her.

She came up to Arjun and asked, "You took the liberty of buying me exotic lingerie?"

"I thought it would give you a heads-up on what's coming up. Want to back out?" he asked gazing into her eyes.

The flaming desire in his eyes created knots in her stomach.

"How did you know my size?" she asked.

"Took a wild guess," he replied.

Tony had arranged for a large SUV. Arjun opened the passenger side front door for Saloni. She was impressed by his chivalrous behaviour. He swiftly moved to the driver's seat.

"Where are we going?" asked Saloni checking herself out in the rear-view mirror.

"Patience sweetheart," replied Arjun.

He played soft and sensuous music to build a romantic atmosphere. He drove for about half an hour and halted in the middle of nowhere.

Saloni looked around, "Are we there?"

"Yes," replied Arjun.

She got out of the car and looked around. It was pitch-dark. The area around the car was clear. She looked at the sky, it was clear. The crescent moon and innumerable stars had brilliantly lit up the sky. She looked at him questioningly.

He carried her and gently seated her on the bonnet of the car and said, "You wanted to see my passionate side. Are you ready?"

Saloni began breathing fast with apprehension. Just then, they heard a sound of a few motorcycles approaching them.

Arjun looked worried. "Looks like we are not alone."

He moved towards Saloni and stood protectively in front of her. Three motorcycles approached them. One of the men removed his helmet. Arjun recognized the man as one of his kidnappers. Arjun scanned the men for weapons. He could sight none. He posed to strike the men. The men had experienced an earlier combat with Arjun and knew that he was capable of knocking them out in a few seconds. They threw a packet at Arjun and took off. Arjun was confused. He picked up the packet and palpated it for its contents. All he could feel were some papers in the packet.

Saloni took the packet from Arjun and opened it. She handed over the contents to Arjun. The packet contained the legal documents that the kidnappers had forced Arjun to sign.

'Why return these?' he wondered.

Saloni looked inside the packet and said, "There's a letter in the packet."

Arjun read the letter.

Dear Arjun,

I am one of your biggest admirers. I had seen you play a courteous host at a few corporate parties. I had seen you perform at the Blueberry Club. Like most young women who know you, I too fell in love with you. I saw you talk to Nysa at my office, you were on your knees. You looked so handsome and adorable. I couldn't put you off my mind. I decided to have you. You never responded to any of my messages. Hence, I kidnapped you. I made you sign the documents so that you have no one to fall back on.

However, fate intervened and you escaped. I followed you to Khajuraho. I was saddened to learn that your sexual preferences did not match mine. However, I still hoped that I was wrong and asked my men to follow you. They confirmed my fears quoting that they had seen you in awkward poses with Shiv outside your hotel rooms.

I respect your sexual preference and have decided to withdraw. Please discard the GPS tracker stuck to the back of your bracelet. In case you decide to straighten up, I would still be interested.

Your biggest fan,
Rajshri Mittal aka Shaina

"Oh my god! Shaina kidnapped and stalked you!" exclaimed Saloni.

Arjun removed his bracelet and found the tracker. He threw it far away. Saloni was fuming with jealousy and passion for Arjun.

"What's the awkward pose with Shiv?" she asked.

"I am not sure but I do remember a man asking if Shiv and I were having a lover's tiff."

"Can't blame him. A lot of people carry that misconception," said Saloni with a mischievous smile.

She couldn't wait any longer. "You were saying something about your passionate side?" she asked rubbing the nape of her neck.

Arjun removed a blindfold from his pocket and fixed it over Saloni's eyes.

"Just a few minutes," he said.

After about ten minutes, he removed Saloni's blindfold. She looked around and was awestruck. A campfire was burning at a distance of a few feet, a comfortable tent was standing near it and a small table with two wine glasses filled with red wine were placed on it. A small vase with a red rose decorated the table and two small chairs were set around it.

While admiring all this, she heard some music. Arjun appeared from behind the SUV. He was topless and wore a pair of suspender pants and a funky hat. He danced to the tune of 'Tempted to touch'. Saloni was turned on by his raunchy moves and his pelvic and chest thrusts. Several times during the dance, he came close to her, but moved away without touching her. She was getting restless and aroused. She couldn't bear to be away from him anymore. His sexy moves with the chair made her go weak in her knees.

He knelt before her and requested her to dance with him; she obliged. The song was Marvin Gaye's 'Let's get it on'. They danced very close to each other. He hugged and felt her. The air was filled with very high passion. The song ended, but Saloni didn't let go of Arjun.

He carried her and gently seated her back on the bonnet and asked, "Are you ready?"

She nodded.

"Okay. You sleep in the car and I will sleep in the tent."

She couldn't believe what she was hearing. Such an anti-climax! She jumped down from the bonnet and punched him in his chest.

"Whoa! Whoa! I was joking. Now I am sure you are ready. Where do you want to start first?"

She didn't wait to answer and began kissing him passionately while moving towards the tent.

At Sanyal House, a police team was gathering information about Bijlani.

"His finger prints have matched with an unknown criminal wanted for murder of a wealthy old couple," said the police chief. "It's a miracle that he let you live, Mr Sanyal. He had killed the old couple ruthlessly."

"No, it's not a miracle. It's because Arjun arrived at the right time. I owe him my life," replied Mr Sanyal.

Shiv expressed his gratitude to Arjun by slightly bowing his head to him. He was glad that his dad had recovered considerably.

"I am surprised that a shrewd person like you did not get Bijlani's credibility checked before employing him," commented the police chief.

"That's because he came from a reliable source," replied Mr Sanyal thoughtfully.

"Who?" asked Shiv.

"Devi ji." Mr Sanyal's reply left everyone stunned.

Mr Ballad had always viewed Shiv as his to be son-in-law. He was having great difficulty in swapping Shiv's image with that of Arjun. However, after observing Saloni's obvious passion and love for Arjun, he had to give in. He went up to Arjun and shook hands with him. He had liked the boy, but never thought of him as his son-in-law. This time, he looked at him from a different angle and surprisingly, developed an instant liking for him. Anyway, it was difficult for anyone to dislike Arjun.

"Dad, Bijlani has stolen all the original artworks from our house," informed Shiv.

"Don't worry son, they all have in-built trackers. They will be found in no time. The entire gang will be exposed," replied Mr Sanyal.

"Do you know where this sculpture is?" asked Shiv, showing a picture of the sculpture that had led them to the treasure.

Mr Sanyal looked at the picture and said, "Oh, this one! It's with Devi ji."

Arjun, Shiv, Saloni and Nysa were shocked.

"Are you sure?" asked Shiv.

"One hundred percent!" replied Mr Sanyal.

Just then, an attendant informed that a man with a parcel was waiting in the living room. All of them went out. The man placed a huge parcel in the living room and gave a letter to Shiv. Shiv opened the letter. It was from Devi ji.

Dear Shiv,

May god bless you! I hope you understand my actions, son. Sometimes, to achieve a big goal, you have to let go of the smaller ones. If I had handed you this sculpture, you would have never gone ahead to find the treasure, the history and glory of Khajuraho. Now, thanks to you, the glory of Khajuraho has been re-established, with evidence. My goal and duty have been fulfilled. You were the destined key-finder in this big plan.

I am sorry Shiv, but your quest for Nysa was nothing but a part of a bigger plan. Just like my role to place Bijlani in your house and coax you to find the treasure is probably a small part of another bigger plan. We all play small roles in the ultimate big game of destiny. The big picture is revealed only after all the jigsaw puzzle pieces fall in their right places. I hope that someday you will forgive me. Thank you for your contribution. Sending the sculpture along.

Your soul guide,
Devi

The police officer looked at the letter and informed them that Ms Devi was a part of the team sent to Khajuraho to decode the script and history of Khajuraho. He switched on the TV.

The news presenter said:

"The discovery of Khajuraho treasure is the most amazing discovery of the century. A panel of several expert historians is being convened. Ms Devi has been unanimously chosen as the expert on Khajuraho history.

"She was the one who entered the snake infested treasure trench and chanted some mantras. To everyone's surprise, the snakes backed off. After this, another trench connecting this one was found. Numerous sculptures, paintings and literature describing and depicting the glorious days of the three dynasties were found in this connecting trench. This discovery is priceless. It is the most astonishing miracle of the century.

"The government has announced a cash reward for Mr Tony D'Souza and his team. Mr D'Souza has provided a list of his team members as beneficiaries of the award. We will keep you posted about this amazing discovery amounting to thousands of crores. A group of men was found unconscious at the treasure sight. A dead gang member was also found in the trench.

"The entire forest is being searched for more treasures. The search has also revealed an ancient cave with some sculptures carved on its walls."

Shiv exchanged a look with Nysa, who smiled back at him.

A few days later, Shiv received another parcel. It contained a sculpture of a man carrying his lover in his arms. The parcel had a card that read:

'Compliments from Tony'.

Shiv smiled and took the parcel to his bedroom. He carried Nysa in his arms, imitating the man in the sculpture, and kissed her.